Thread of Suspicion

I. D.

DATE DUE

	83065	

Thread of Suspicion

Jane Peart

Fleming H. Revell
A Division of Baker Book House
Grand Rapids, Michigan 49516

Published by Fleming H. Revell
a division of Baker Book House Company
P.O. Box 6287, Grand Rapids, MI 49516-6287

Printed in the United States of America

Library of Congress Cataloging-in-Publication Data

Peart, Jane.
    Thread of suspicion / Jane Peart.
      p. cm.
    ISBN 0-8007-5676-2
    1. Title.
    PS3566.E238T48 1998
    813'.54—dc21   98-8818

Scripture quotations are from the King James Version of the Bible.

For current information about all releases from Baker Book House, visit our web site:

http://www.bakerbooks.com

Prologue

August 20, 1893

It is difficult to imagine I have been the dining room hostess at Seaview Inn, this small hotel in the popular English resort town, for two years already. Today, an unexpected offer changed my life.

Shortly after the lunch hour, the manager, Mr. Robley, beckoned me and in a confidential manner told me one of our guests, Mr. Gervase Montgomery, wished to speak to me.

I knew who Mr. Montgomery was because he had been a guest at the inn several times in the past year. I had noticed him not only for his distinguished appearance but also for his pleasant personality. He always treated the members of the staff, the waiters, and the chambermaids courteously. There was not the least bit of arrogance or condescension in his manner, nor did he demand unusual services as many gentlemen of his class did.

He had always been cordial when he came in for meals and early on addressed me by my name. He usually asked for the same table at the window. He was polite and most generous with gratuities to his waiter. I had occasionally been aware of his observing me, especially when I was conversing with other guests. In the afternoons, when I provided piano music during the tea hour, he was always an attentive audience. Still, I couldn't imagine what reason he would have to see me privately.

After lunch, when the last few guests had left the dining room, I went to the ladies room off the lobby to check my appearance. I had been on duty since eleven o'clock and had not had a chance to look in a mirror since early morning. I made a quick survey, smoothing my hair, which, because of its tendency to curl, I wear drawn back into a high coil, more suited to me than the current popularity of fringes and crimping.

In spite of my limited wardrobe, I have always prided myself on having a flair for fashion. Today was no exception. Although simple in design, my dress was given a certain panache by the white linen Byron collar I had added. The color, heather-blue, was becoming to my dark hair and eyes. Satisfied, I then hurried down the hall to one of the small parlors where Mr. Robley had indicated Mr. Montgomery would be waiting.

When I entered, Mr. Montgomery stood and bowed slightly, again impressing me with his courteousness. He was well groomed, expensively tailored, his dark hair silvered at the temples. He had strong features and, I thought, kind eyes. He gestured toward one of the armchairs in the bow-windowed alcove and waited until I was seated before sitting down opposite me. He then proceeded to offer me a most unexpected position, the unique circumstances of which he described.

It seems his niece, Allegra Selkirk, is confined to a wheelchair after being involved in a carriage accident in which both her parents were killed. Her mother was thrown out of the vehicle and was fatally injured. Her father lay unconscious and dying near Allegra, who was pinned underneath one of the broken wheels close by. The horses, trapped in their harnesses by the overturned vehicle, kicked and struggled.

Although it was later determined she had sustained only minor injuries, Allegra had remained helpless there until rescuers finally arrived and were able to reach and extricate the victims.

Before the accident, Allegra was a healthy, active young woman, an accomplished horseback rider. However, since then, Allegra has not been able to move her legs, to stand or to walk, although the doctors cannot find any physical reason why she should be paralyzed. Even more mystifying than the paralysis is her other symptom. Allegra has not spoken since the time of the accident.

Mr. Montgomery let me absorb this dramatic story for a few minutes; then he asked me if I was familiar with the writings of an Austrian doctor, Sigmund Freud. I told him I was not. He went on to tell me that this physician has put forth a new theory that sometimes an emotional shock can manifest itself physically with no apparent medical cause. He explained that

7

Dr. Freud calls it hysterical illness, real to the patient but quite without foundation medically. Usual methods of treatment are of no avail in these circumstances.

In quest of help for his niece, he recently traveled to Vienna to consult with Dr. Freud, and he is now convinced Allegra suffers from this kind of illness. Mr. Montgomery believes that what happened at the accident, the deaths of both parents, has traumatized Allegra. He feels that in order to get well she must get beyond her prolonged grieving and what Dr. Freud terms survivor's guilt, a kind of self-punishment that is blocking her recovery.

This is where I come in. Mr. Montgomery wants someone who also believes in this possibility to be with his niece. With the right companion to encourage her, he hopes Allegra can gradually regain her health, mobility, and speech.

Allegra is his sister Henrietta's only child, and she is very dear to him. He confided that no one else in his late brother-in-law's family shares his conviction that she can recover. Allegra is surrounded by relatives, staff, and servants, including a personal maid, who treat her like a hopeless invalid. They pamper her, waiting on her hand and foot so she has no incentive to try to do anything for herself. Mr. Montgomery said he has the unfortunate suspicion it is to their advantage she remain helpless. His remark struck me as very odd indeed.

But my greater astonishment is the question of why he has selected me as a possible companion for his niece. I am neither a nurse nor a governess. I have no experience with illness. Nothing in my background has prepared me for the position he wants me to fill.

Perhaps Mr. Montgomery overheard me conversing with some of our French guests, of whom there have been many, and therefore deems me better educated than I really am. Little does he know that I was left an orphan at age six and was reared by my father's two maiden aunts who run a small school for young ladies. Nor does he know that I spent my childhood summers in France and learned French from my grandmother, Madeline.

When I attempted to tell Mr. Montgomery of my lack of qualifications as a companion to his invalid niece, he brushed away my objections and continued as if I had not even spoken. Again I tried to dissuade him, saying that he didn't really know me. At that point, he held up one hand, as if to ward off further protests. He said he had made inquiries, and he was fully satisfied that I was the right choice. I wonder what kind of inquiries Mr. Montgomery has made about me and of whom?

He then continued, saying he would pay me double what I was making at the inn and assuring me my main duty would be to be available to Allegra. I would have my own comfortable suite of rooms in a beautiful house in scenic surroundings and plenty of free time to pursue my own interests—pursuits, he suggested, I might try to persuade Allegra to join. He concluded by saying, what she needs most is companionship and someone young to encourage her to get well, to emerge from her cocoon of misery and mourning. At nineteen, Allegra has her whole life ahead of her. Mr. Montgomery said I should try to find the cause, whatever it is, that is keeping her a self-imposed recluse and invalid.

Mr. Montgomery's concern for his niece was evident, and I was deeply moved by his sincerity. I could see he loves her very much and is extremely worried about her condition.

As I look back on this scene, I must admit my curiosity about his niece has been aroused, and the unexpected opportunity to widen my experience is enticing. The salary he mentioned could not help but influence someone who has a longing for travel and adventure. The job at Seaview has lost its novelty and often seems humdrum. So, in less than half an hour, arrangements were made. At the end of the summer season, when the Seaview Inn closes for the winter, I will travel to Dorset and begin my employment as companion to Allegra Selkirk.

Before Mr. Montgomery departed, he gave me an envelope containing several pound notes to cover my train fare and traveling expenses, and the address of his London club where he could be reached.

Finally, he handed me a card with the name of the Selkirk estate—Hope's End. When I first saw the name, I felt a strange sort of premonition, which I quickly dismissed. I am too filled with excitement and the anticipation of an interesting change to do more than think it odd.

$\mathcal{N}$ell entered the second-class compartment of the train and was glad to see she was the only occupant. She took off her coat and gloves and settled herself by the window. She removed her hat, newly trimmed with wide Alsatian ribbons, placing it carefully on the seat beside her.

She had been so anxious to be off on her new venture that it had been difficult to listen patiently to Aunt Emma and Aunt Hester's last-minute warnings about travel. It was almost as if they had forgotten that even as a child she had set out on trips alone, dividing her time between the school year in England with them and summers in France with her grandmother. Had they also forgotten that she had earned her own living for the past six years, first as a French tutor, then as an apprentice to a milliner and a sales clerk in a dress shop before her job at the Seaview Inn?

She loved her two aunts dearly and was grateful to them for giving her a home after her parents died. She appreciated that they had tried to bring her up as a proper English lady, even changing her French name, Danielle, one they decided was too foreign, to the more acceptable Nell.

Maybe it was this veneer that had led Gervase Montgomery to select her for his niece's companion. Whatever his reason, Nell was excited. At last, her curiosity to explore another aspect of life would be satisfied.

The conductor walked down the platform, shutting compartment doors with a clang as he came. He peered into Nell's, looked around, and, seeing she was alone, tipped his cap. "Enjoy your trip, miss. There'll be two stops before we reach Hope's End."

That name, Nell thought with a little quiver of distaste. She knew many English estates had unusual names, but this one had a singularly strange connotation. Mr. Montgomery had told her the trip would take about three hours and that someone from the Selkirk household would meet her. He would write ahead to inform his late sister's brother-in-law, Desmond, when she would be arriving.

Nell felt the train start to move. She was on her way. The first half hour, she spent most of the time looking out the window at the passing landscape—hills shrouded in mist and picturesque villages nestled in deep valleys. She had usually traveled in the opposite direction, going first to Dover and then taking the boat train to France. Soon, however, her thoughts turned inward to where she was going and what she might possibly find upon her arrival.

Gervase Montgomery's description of his niece intrigued her. Because of her own experience, Nell could relate to Allegra's having been orphaned. Of course, Nell had been much younger than Allegra; she was only three years old at her mother's death and six when her rather distant, widowed father died. She had not had years of knowing them, loving them, being close to them as evidently Allegra had with her parents. Even so, there was that basic common ground. She hoped that might serve as a bond to help them develop a friendship and to accomplish what Gervase wanted so badly—Allegra's full recovery. However, Nell realized she had taken on a big responsibility.

Nell felt a nervous flutter in her stomach then decided it must be hunger. She had been too excited to eat much of the hearty breakfast her aunts had served. Now, however, she felt hungry and opened the small wicker basket Aunt Emma had handed her just before she left. She selected a lemon muffin and a small, tart apple. Outside, the countryside seemed to spin by and, before she knew it, she felt the train slowing. Perhaps they were coming to the first stop the conductor had mentioned.

This was the midpoint of the journey. There would be another ninety minutes in the confinement of her compartment before she reached her destination.

When the train pulled into the station, Nell decided to get out for a breath of fresh air and a little exercise. As she stepped out onto the platform, she saw a man striding toward her. Gervase Montgomery! What was he doing here? She stood quite still as he approached.

"Good day, Miss Winston," he said cordially. "I can understand your surprise at seeing me. However, some new developments have arisen in the Selkirk household for which I should prepare you."

"I hope it is nothing distressing, Mr. Montgomery; your niece is not worse or . . ." Nell left the sentence dangling uncertainly.

"No, no, it is not Allegra. Unfortunately it is my sister's brother-in-law, Desmond Selkirk. We have had a quarrel. A serious one. Quite frankly, he was angry when I told him I had engaged you as Allegra's companion, which is entirely within my rights as her guardian. He took offense, saying I was trying to usurp his authority in his own home, which is nonsense. I am simply concerned about the welfare of my niece. Until she is twenty-one, I have the duty to do whatever I feel in my judgment is in her best interest."

"You mean, Mr. Selkirk doesn't approve of my coming?"

"It is nothing personal, Miss Winston, I assure you. Desmond likes having everything in his control. He was named the executor of his brother's estate, so, after Matthew's death, he moved into the home that is Allegra's by inheritance and simply took over." Gervase's mouth tightened, and his face seemed to set in grim lines. "With Allegra in the condition she was in after the accident, it seemed at the time the best arrangement. Now, however, it makes my situation difficult."

Perplexed, Nell waited for him to continue. Perhaps she was simply to take the next train back to her aunts, dismissed from her new position before ever having taken it.

"To put it quite bluntly, Miss Winston, I am no longer welcome in Selkirk's house, nor can I see my niece. Therefore, you have become my emissary—my eyes and ears, in other words—to observe everything that concerns Allegra in that household and to give me a full report."

A look of intense concern passed over Mr. Montgomery's face. "This has necessitated my investigating some legal matters regarding my niece's situation. Of course, my sister and her husband had no idea they would die so young, and some of their wishes were not articulated as well as one could wish. At any rate, I may have to be out of the country for some time. This, I'm afraid, puts a heavier burden on you, Miss Winston. I want you to write me regularly, giving me a full report of your impressions, observations, anything that might seem important to you about my niece's care, the household, her emotional state. This is what Dr. Freud advocates in cases in which a physical condition may have an emotional basis. Since I am not allowed to do this myself, I shall have to rely on you, Miss Winston. You have my address at the London club; is that correct?"

Nell nodded. She was bewildered at Mr. Montgomery's unexpected appearance and by his uncharacteristic demeanor. He had lost his usual dignified, calm nature. He was obviously upset about his quarrel with his late sister's brother-in-law and its possible repercussions. Just then the train's warning whistle shrilled in the morning air. Its imminent departure left no time for questions or further explanations. Mr. Montgomery placed his hand under Nell's elbow and escorted her back to her compartment. He closed the door and, leaning in through the window, told her, " I trust you will be discreet about this meeting and will report to me anything suspicious or untoward you sense in the Selkirks' home that could be in any way detrimental to Allegra's recovery. I feel my niece's very existence is at stake. That's why I need someone of your integrity as my ally. I have full confidence in you, Miss Winston."

The train began to move slowly. Nell had a dozen conflicting thoughts, things she would have liked to discuss with Gervase Montgomery, but already the opportunity was gone as his tall figure grew smaller and was finally lost to sight.

Nell thought of Gervase Montgomery's parting words, wishing she had the same confidence in herself. The position she had suddenly taken now seemed a great deal more complicated. She thought of what he had said about no longer being welcome at Hope's End. Did that mean that neither would she be welcome there? The train gathered speed, hurtling down the track, carrying her nearer and nearer to whatever awaited her.

The unexpected meeting with Gervase Montgomery had been disturbing. He had not even hinted at these developments when he first interviewed her. Perhaps this meeting had been planned when it would be too late for her to change her mind about accepting the position, which seemed to have changed in nature. From simply being a companion she had been turned into a spy for Gervase in a household where he was unwelcome. This meeting gave their arrangement an element of secrecy she had not bargained for, and that made her extremely uncomfortable.

What would she find at the Selkirks'? She had imagined herself employing some of her natural abilities honed by the previous jobs she had held. She was by nature a sympathetic person, a good listener, and she prided herself on being responsible and dependable. Now she was not at all sure these were the skills she would need in a difficult situation made even more so by these new circumstances.

For the rest of the journey, she gazed out the window at the landscape, too preoccupied and a bit troubled   15 to be aware of the other brief stop. The train rattled over a viaduct then rushed down a hillside and came to a stop in front of a neat stucco and timbered station house.

Nell thought back to the previous Sunday's church service. The minister of the small congregation, no doubt nudged by one of Nell's aunts, who had told him she was leaving on a trip, had chosen a prayer for travelers at the close of his sermon. Nell remembered it now. "Grant to all travelers protection from danger, accompany them by thy holy angels that they may arrive at their destination safely and be kept out of harm's way."

As she collected her belongings and prepared to leave the train, Nell hoped that the prayer had indeed been meant for her.

2

A light rain, no more than a mist, was falling as Nell stepped out of the compartment onto the platform and looked around anxiously for whomever the Selkirks had sent to meet her.

The few passengers who had left the train the same time as she had quickly dispersed, departing with friends into waiting carriages. Nell found herself alone on the deserted platform. A dreadful thought occurred. Could the Selkirks have been so displeased at Gervase's hiring her that they deliberately ignored her arrival? Just as other equally unnerving possibilities took seed in her imagination, Nell saw a small, one-horse trap pull to a stop at the side of the station house. A young man jumped out, tied the horse to the hitching post, and walked onto the platform. He glanced around; then, seeing Nell was the only person there, he tipped his billed cap and came forward. "Miss Winston?"

"Yes," she said, relieved yet puzzled. Was he part of the estate staff or a member of the family? It was hard to tell from his attire. He could have been a country squire in his belted tweed jacket and riding boots. He was certainly not a liveried coachman, and his manner was too confident to be a trained servant. She took a second look. Perhaps in his early thirties, the man had a ruddy complexion, strong features, and sharp, clear blue eyes.

"These yours, miss?" He pointed to the two suitcases, the valise, and the hatbox at her feet.

"Yes." As he reached for them, she added quickly, "I'll carry the hatbox."

He looked at her with an amused smile. "Is this all?"

"No, my trunk is over there." Nell pointed to her small, humpbacked trunk—the sole piece remaining on the luggage cart. It looked as lonely and abandoned as she had felt a few minutes before.

"I'll get it," he said. Then almost as an afterthought he answered her unspoken question. "I'm Hugh Douglass, the stable master. There was no one else to send."

A cryptic comment. Most gentry households had staffs of at least twenty with precise duties for each one. It seemed strange that the Selkirks should send the stable manager. Perhaps it was a subtle way of letting her know she was not an invited guest but merely an unwanted employee.

Douglass carried the trunk easily and buckled it onto the back of the trap. He assisted Nell up, then got in beside her and took up the reins. He gave a light flick of his whip to the horse, and they started off.

The sky was overcast with threatening clouds. Nell, thinking of her refurbished bonnet, wondered if it would rain before they reached the Selkirks' house and ventured to ask, "Is it far?"

"No, miss, about two miles," Douglass replied. He gave her a swift look, and again a smile tugged at his mouth. "We'll be there soon enough."

Certainly this man was not talkative, and, equally clear, he had no intention of filling her in on many of the things she would have liked to know about the Selkirks' establishment. His status, for instance. Another sidelong glance confirmed her first impression. Hugh Douglass was undeniably handsome, his nose nobly arched, his jaw and chin strong. Stubborn? He handled the horse expertly as was natural in his position as stable master. But how did he fit into the household?

They left the main road and turned off onto a narrow lane banded on both sides by deep woods. The sky overhead was darkening rapidly, the clouds increasingly ominous. Before Nell could get too worried about the possibility of a downpour, they came to black iron gates that opened onto a gravel drive winding slowly uphill.

The approach to the mansion tunneled through shaggy rhododendrons on either side, forming so dense a screen that the house was obscured from sight until they rounded the last bend. It seemed to appear suddenly—a huge, gray stone structure set against a gray-purple sky.

Suddenly, Nell was struck by a fanciful thought. It might have seemed bizarre had not Gervase Montgomery confided some of his suspicions about his niece's situation. The Selkirk mansion reminded Nell of a fortresslike castle. Was Allegra like the mythical Briar Rose, a captive princess cut off from the outside world? Were the Selkirks guarding Allegra here or imprisoning her? Nell pushed away her questions. From childhood, her aunts had tried to discourage her from imaginative fancies. But somehow the thought lingered.

"Here you are, miss," Douglass announced as he pulled to a stop in front of the house. "I'll get down your things and bring them in. You go on up. Just pull the bell. They're expectin' you." She caught the slightest burr of a Scots accent in his voice. *Douglass—of course, a fine old Scottish name.*

She got down and started up the stone steps to the front door. It opened before she got to the top. A thin, grave-faced man, with bushy white sideburns and little hair on top of his head, held the door wide for her to enter. He bowed stiffly. "Good afternoon, miss. I'm Farnsworth."

"I'm Miss Winston."

"Yes, miss. I'll let Mrs. Selkirk know you've come," he said, then disappeared down the hall leaving Nell alone in the foyer.

It was splendid with mellow paneling. A staircase of polished wood led up to the second floor; at the landing was a magnificent stained glass window, which in sunlight must come alive with rich color. There was a carved table flanked by two high-backed chairs with tapestried covers. Oriental rugs were spread on the parquet floor.

From what Gervase Montgomery had told her, the young Selkirks had traveled widely and had brought back many beautiful things for the house they loved; they also had entertained frequently and enjoyed sharing their home with others. However, for all the luxuriousness of the interior, Nell was conscious of a disturbing sensation. The minute she stepped inside she had felt something indiscernible, a kind of stirring unease, as if something was hovering over the house.

She had no time to analyze her feeling because the butler was back to tell her that Mrs. Selkirk was waiting for her. Nell followed Farnsworth into an ornately decorated room. It seemed unusually dark until she realized the day outside had darkened rapidly and the gas lamps had not yet been lighted. At her entrance, a plump, blond woman rose from a cushioned settee and came forward, extending a heavily ringed hand to her. "Well, Miss Winston, you've come," she said breathlessly.

That seemed obvious, but Nell replied politely, "Yes, Mrs. Selkirk, I'm pleased to meet you."

"Well, well, I hope it wasn't too difficult a journey. Have you had tea? Or do you want to meet Allegra right away since that's what you've come for, isn't it?"

The woman seemed flustered, almost confused. Her agitation made Nell feel even more insecure. Before she could answer that she would very much like to meet Allegra, Mrs. Selkirk rushed on. "Oh, no, that won't be possible—at least not right away. Her doctor is with her now. Perhaps we should have tea here." Over Nell's shoulder, she nodded to the butler, who had remained standing in the doorway. "Farnsworth, bring us in tea."

"Very well, madam."

After he left, Mrs. Selkirk fluttered her hand vaguely in the direction of a round, velvet chair. "Do sit down, Miss Winston. Was your trip difficult? Oh, but then I've already asked you that, haven't I? I do hate to travel myself, and so I imagine it is the same for everyone."

Nell started to take a seat, pulling off her gloves as she did so. Why was Mrs. Selkirk so nervous? Had her coming caused this much consternation among the Selkirks? Nell did not have a chance to follow this line of thinking further, for at that moment, Mrs. Selkirk's elaborately coiffed head inclined slightly toward the door through which male voices and footsteps could be heard.

"Oh, dear!" She gave a spontaneous little gasp, her fingers pressed to her open mouth. "Here come my husband and Dr. Herbert now."

Nell turned in the direction Mrs. Selkirk was looking and watched two men enter.

"Desmond, dear, Miss Winston has arrived."

The man she addressed halted on the threshold. Desmond Selkirk was an imposing figure, his reddish-brown hair thick and wavy, his features well molded. He might have been considered handsome by some, if it had not been for his eyes—blue steel, now regarding Nell appraisingly. The younger man, dark-haired, with a well-trimmed mustache and beard, must be Dr. Herbert.

"Ah, indeed, Miss Winston," Selkirk said with a heartiness Nell felt struck a false note. "This is Dr. Herbert, Allegra's physician, Miss Winston." He tapped the doctor's arm. "Gervase's protégé, you know, the one I told you about."

Nell stiffened, indignant at the description.

Frowning, the doctor repeated her name. "Miss Winston."

Then he turned to Selkirk and smiled. "Ah, yes, the young woman Gervase hired."

Selkirk's mouth tightened, and he nodded curtly. "The same."

"I was just going to take Miss Winston up to meet Allegra," Mrs. Selkirk said, her voice hesitant.

"I don't think that's advisable, Mrs. Selkirk," Dr. Herbert said authoritatively. "I have just come from examining Allegra, and I find her very weak today. Not at all up to seeing anyone, especially a stranger."

The doctor then turned to Nell. "I'm sure you can understand, Miss Winston. However good your intentions might be, introducing a new person into Allegra's small circle can be disturbing to someone in her emotional and physical condition."

Not knowing exactly how to respond, Nell merely nodded and murmured, "Of course." She was already seething inwardly at the way she was being treated. She was being made to feel, intentionally or not, an odd hybrid, neither an invited guest nor a servant. An awkward silence followed.

Dr. Herbert came over to Nell. "We must have a talk, Miss Winston, before you take up your duties with Allegra—whatever they will be." His voice had a sarcastic edge. "I have been a family friend for many years, as well as her attending physician since the unfortunate accident. There is much I could tell you in preparation to your becoming her companion—as that is what I surmise you are intended to be." His tone sharpened. "I caution you not to move too quickly in anything you may have in mind to suggest. Allegra is in a very fragile condition, and I would certainly want to be apprised of any changes in her regimen."

Nell simply nodded. Dr. Herbert smiled down at her, his teeth white and square against his swarthy skin. Nell felt an instant dislike.

"Have Miss Winston shown to her room, Millicent," Mr.

Selkirk said in a tone that sounded more like a command than a suggestion.

Mrs. Selkirk seemed startled. "We were about to have tea, Desmond," she began. Then, darting a quick look at him, she said to Nell, "But then I suppose you would prefer to have it upstairs in your room. You must be tired, and perhaps you would like to rest and refresh yourself a bit before—"

"We dine at seven, Miss Winston," Mr. Selkirk interrupted rudely.

Quickly, Mrs. Selkirk went to the tapestry bellpull and jerked it. Farnsworth reappeared with a silver tea service on a tray. Mrs. Selkirk motioned to the table in front of the fireplace.

"Set that down, Farnsworth, then go and ask Mrs. Russell—no, no, Jewel will do. Tell her we need her to take Miss Winston upstairs."

Nell was beginning to feel her presence was causing no end of trouble, and certainly no one did the least to make her feel more at ease. Mr. Selkirk was openly scowling; the doctor was standing at the marble mantelpiece, his back to the room, rubbing his hands as if warming them at the glowing fire, ignoring the flurry behind him. Nell almost felt pity for Mrs. Selkirk, who seemed at a total loss of how to manage this situation.

Thankfully, within a few minutes, the housemaid, Jewel, a sturdy, rosy-cheeked girl in a gray striped dress, white ruffled apron, and cap, entered the room. She dropped a curtsey to Nell. "If you'll come this way, miss."

Glad to be out of the room bristling with tension, Nell followed Jewel into the hall. Nell's suitcases, valise, trunk, and hatbox were at the bottom of the staircase. She stopped to retrieve them.

"Here, miss, let me. I'll have someone carry up your trunk."

"I can handle the hatbox," Nell said, and they proceeded up the steps.

Halfway to the landing, Jewel stopped and whispered, "Here comes Mrs. Russell, the housekeeper."

Nell looked up. A woman, dressed in black, descended the next flight of steps. Reaching the landing, she halted in a posture of austere dignity. She looked at Jewel pointedly.

"Mrs. Russell," Jewel began, "this is Miss Allegra's new—" then as if not knowing what title to give Nell, she glanced from one to the other before saying, "This is Miss Winston; I'm just taking her to her room."

Abreast of her now, Nell observed that the housekeeper was about fifty. A white lace cap covered iron gray hair. She had a long, thin nose, keen eyes, and a haughty demeanor. Nell was well aware of the important position housekeepers held and how acceptance by her might set the attitude of the household staff. She held out her hand and smiled pleasantly. "Good afternoon, Mrs. Russell. I'm happy to meet you."

"Good afternoon." The housekeeper inclined her head in the manner of royalty speaking to a subject. "Go ahead, Jewel; I'll escort Miss Winston to her rooms." Jewel scurried off, and Mrs. Russell turned and led the way to the top of the stairway, then along the corridor to where Jewel stood at an open door. Mrs. Russell gestured for Nell to precede her. "I think you'll be quite comfortable here, Miss Winston. This is the sitting room, and your bedroom adjoins it. Miss Allegra's suite is just down the hall."

The room into which Nell was ushered was pleasant and comfortably furnished. There was an armchair in front of a small fireplace, and a desk and chair in a windowed alcove. Jewel trundled in with the suitcases and took them into the bedroom. As Nell looked around appreciatively, Mrs. Russell dismissed Jewel. Turning to Nell, she pursed her lips for a moment as if considering what she was going to say.

"Since you have just come and have hardly had time to become acquainted either with the family or the rest of the staff, there are a few things about this establishment it might help you to know, Miss Winston." She hesitated a moment before continuing. "This is not the usual kind of household, mainly because of Miss Allegra. She is an invalid, and everything revolves around her. She is not to be upset, disturbed, or agitated in any way. It is absolutely essential she remain calm. These are Dr. Herbert's direct orders."

A strange expression came over Mrs. Russell's face. She started to say something more, then appeared to change her mind. She walked over to the window and, choosing her words carefully, said, "I came here with the Selkirks after the accident. As did the cook. We have found this to be an entirely different household than our former experience with our employers in their London home. There are rarely guests, and there is very little entertaining. I hope you are prepared for this kind of situation, Miss Winston." She paused, as if to emphasize her next words: "We have all had to adjust. You would be advised to keep that always in mind too."

"I have every reason to believe I can and will adjust, Mrs. Russell."

The housekeeper gave Nell a long, penetrating look, then swept out of the room, leaving Nell more puzzled than ever about Hope's End.

*A*fter Mrs. Russell's departure, Nell walked through the rooms of her suite several times. She did not feel at all tired from her train trip. In fact, she felt exhilarated by the challenge of her new situation.

Her trunk had not yet been brought up, so in the meantime, she would arrange some of her personal belongings. She emptied her valise, taking out her toilette articles—her hairbrush and hand mirror, a box of bath powder, the rose water and glycerine skin lotion. She removed the cap from a bottle of violet cologne and took a long, fragrant whiff. It had been a farewell gift from the waitresses at Seaview Inn. What a contrast her chilly reception here had been from the warm welcome she had received from the entire staff at Seaview from her very first day. Ah, well, it was Allegra's acceptance that was important. From what the housekeeper had said, everything revolved around her. And Nell had yet to meet her.

Nell opened one of her suitcases and took from it the items she brought with her wherever she traveled: two small photographs of her parents, one of Grandmere standing under the rose trellis in her pension garden, and the small, velvet-lined jewelry box that played a sweet tune when the lid was lifted. Other than the pendant watch and small gold heart earrings she always wore, Nell owned only a few pieces that had sentimental value—a cameo brooch that had belonged to her mother, a pair of pearl stud earrings, and a seed pearl necklace.

She took out her Bible and concordance and set them on her bedside table. From her early childhood years, during winter months spent with her aunts, Scripture reading before bedtime had been the nightly routine, a practice Nell still continued.

While she was arranging her things, Nell wondered about the young woman whose companion she had been hired to be. She was anxious to meet her, to develop a trusting friendship so that she could find a way to help her. Maybe the fact that Nell understood what being an orphan was like would bind them in a special way.

From somewhere deep in the house, Nell heard the resonant sound of a gong. She checked her watch. Five minutes to seven. From the way Mr. Selkirk had announced the dinner hour, Nell sensed punctuality was important in this house. She certainly did not want to be late and make a bad impression her first night.

With a quick look in the mirror, she decided her gray traveling suit edged with darker gray velvet was stylish and entirely suitable—unless the Selkirks dressed formally for dinner. But if they did, surely Mrs. Russell would have mentioned it. Hadn't the housekeeper informed her that Hope's End was not like most country homes where such social amenities were maintained? Remembering the other things Mrs. Russell had said, Nell felt a tiny sliver of apprehension. Perhaps it was what the housekeeper had left unsaid that might be even more important.

The double doors to the dining room were open, and Nell crossed the hall and entered to find everyone else already seated. Mrs. Selkirk indicated the chair to her left, and Nell slipped into it just as Mr. Selkirk lowered his head and intoned what Nell supposed was grace but sounded more like a gruff mumble.

Jewel and Farnsworth came in from the kitchen carrying a tureen and soup plates. While they served, Nell glanced around the table. Dr. Herbert was seated at the place usually allotted a guest of honor, at Mr. Selkirk's right. Opposite the doctor sat a lady of uncertain age, whose sharp features were prominent in her thin face. Her hair was arranged in a frizzy fringe, a style becoming only to the very young. It had also undergone a poor henna job, and the dark roots could be clearly seen. She might once have been pretty, but now the relentless progress of time showed in her face. Traces of discontent about her mouth gave her a petulant look.

"I don't believe you've met Miss Benedict, Miss Winston," Mrs. Selkirk said in a quiet tone.

"Of course, she hasn't, Millicent!" her husband barked.

Mrs. Selkirk gave a small jump at her husband's harsh rebuke and lowered her voice even further. "Clarise was Allegra's governess before the accident . . . and afterwards, she stayed on . . ." Her voice trailed off, then she added, "They are, of course, very fond of each other."

Miss Benedict simpered and glanced over at Dr. Herbert as if for approval, but he was studying the contents of his wineglass and not looking at her at all. Nell saw Miss Benedict blush, and she scarcely acknowledged Nell's smile and nod.

Another challenge, Nell thought, as she picked up her spoon and started on her soup. It was delicious, a clear broth with chicken and mushrooms, but it was hard to enjoy it in the strained atmosphere. While the two men carried on a conversation, ignoring the others, Nell had a chance to observe her host, Allegra's uncle and Gervase Montgomery's nemesis.

Selkirk was the image of a successful man—a man of the

city rather than a country squire. He was the type of man who put on airs, who felt superior because of his position. He consumed his food ravenously and refilled his wineglass frequently. Nell thought his face looked unhealthily flushed, the broken veins in his cheeks giving it color. She had already noticed the coldness of his eyes, but now she observed how his mouth was inclined to sneer when he spoke. His attitude toward his wife distressed Nell; he seemed to let no opportunity pass to embarrass or hurt her. Nell despised people who took advantage of those weaker or unable to defend themselves. Before the soup course ended, she came to dislike Desmond Selkirk thoroughly.

Nell's stomach began to tighten with tension. Poor Mrs. Selkirk was toying nervously with her silverware, merely touching her food as one course followed the next. Selkirk and the doctor voiced their opinions loudly. Nell observed how the physician's views dominated even Selkirk. She found them offensive, tinged as they were with cynicism. He made several references to new "outlandish" ideas "flying abroad nowadays without any scientific or medical basis to validate them made by inexperienced experimenters, or worse, charlatans." Nell felt this was directed expressly for her benefit so that she would know what Dr. Herbert thought of the theory Gervase Montgomery had brought back from Vienna and applied to Allegra's condition.

Farnsworth was busy at the sideboard when there was the sound of high-pitched voices and scuffling in the hall outside the dining room.

Mr. Selkirk flung down his napkin and half rose from his chair. "What the blazes is going on?" he shouted. "What is that racket all about?"

Mrs. Selkirk turned pale and pushed back her chair. She started to get up just as Jewel appeared at the dining room entrance, holding the arm of a disheveled old woman who was trying to pull away from her.

"Oh, dear, it's Nanny!" Mrs. Selkirk sighed and threw a

worried glance toward her husband at the other end of the table.

"What is she doing down here?" demanded Selkirk, his face turning an angry red.

"I really can't say—" faltered Mrs. Selkirk, her feeble response drowned out by the querulous voice of the old woman referred to as Nanny.

"Let me go, girl! I want my supper, and I want to see this newcomer with my own eyes."

Suddenly Nell was aware of all eyes upon *her.*

Mrs. Selkirk looked almost frantic. "I don't know what possessed her tonight. She usually has her meals on a tray in her room." For a moment, Nell thought Mrs. Selkirk might be reduced to tears.

"Millicent, for heaven's sake, do something!" roared Mr. Selkirk.

"Yes, yes, Desmond," she said, and finally directed the maid who was also looking for help, "Let her go, Jewel, and set another place at the table. Next to me will be fine."

To the old woman, she spoke placatingly, "Come along, Nanny, do sit down. It's all right." She led her gently while Farnsworth pulled out a chair and eased her down into it.

"This is Miss Winston, Nanny." Over her head she explained to Nell, "Mavis Maybank was Allegra's nurse and her mother's before that." She shook her head. "Devoted but just a wee bit—" She tapped a forefinger to her temple.

Nell looked over at Nanny and smiled. "How do you do."

The woman's beady, dark eyes, shiny as shoe buttons, scrutinized her. "What did you say your name was?" she asked in a sharp voice.

"Winston. Nell Winston."

"And you've come to—" Her gnomelike face scrunched into a wrinkled expression. "Just what is it you've come to do?"

"Hrmmph." This from Mr. Selkirk. A suppressed laugh? Nell glanced in his direction and saw what she could only describe as a smirk on the doctor's face as well. She lifted her chin a little and replied to Nanny's question with as much quiet dignity as she could muster.

"I've come to be Allegra's companion and, I hope, her friend."

Nanny's little mouth pursed as if she were turning this over in her mind. Farnsworth and Jewel went on serving.

If it had not been that Nell was used to older folks, having dealt with many such guests at Seaview Inn to say nothing of her elderly great-aunts, Nanny's constant staring at her might have made her terribly uncomfortable. As it was, she tried to engage her several times in conversation but discovered Nanny was hard of hearing, making her efforts quite futile. However, Nell did smile at her often and thought, at last, she saw a glimmer of acceptance in Nanny's eyes.

Over dessert, Nell was surprised to hear talk about the Selkirks' daughter. It seemed Felicity was expected home from boarding school for the Christmas holidays. Nell had not even known they had a daughter. This was the first mention of her.

"When do you expect the young lady?" Dr. Herbert asked.

"In a couple months or so," Mrs. Selkirk replied. "She has an invitation to visit a friend for a fortnight before coming here. She wrote that there will be a ball and several parties celebrating the brother's return from India. Such gala occasions she did not want to miss."

"Your daughter is becoming quite a social butterfly," Dr. Herbert commented with a smile. "And growing beautiful as well from my last glimpse of her this summer."

At the doctor's remark, Nell noticed Miss Benedict stiffen visibly. Her fingers gripped the stem of her wineglass tightly. A flood of color rose from her neck up into her cheeks. It was not a becoming blush. Rather, it gave her face a blotched look.

Dr. Herbert turned to Mr. Selkirk. "I imagine you're going

to have quite a time, Desmond, keeping hordes of suitors at bay when your lovely Felicity is in residence."

Mr. Selkirk's brows came together, and he glared at the doctor. "I have plans for my daughter, Colin, and I don't brook fools who come with empty promises and pockets."

Dr. Herbert gave a brief, harsh laugh. "Then you don't believe in romantic courtships, Desmond?"

"I run a tight ship as we used to say when I was an ensign in the Royal Navy. Only those I approve of will be allowed to come courting Felicity."

Again Dr. Herbert seemed amused. He raised one eyebrow. "Haven't you ever heard the old adage that 'love laughs at locksmiths'?"

Nell's hands clenched the napkin in her lap. She was chilled by this exchange between the two men. She had never heard a conversation concerning someone's daughter more lacking in affection. She could not help but pity Felicity.

At last the meal came to an end. Mrs. Selkirk rose, as did Miss Benedict. Nanny was led away and taken upstairs by Jewel. The two men remained at the table with the decanter of brandy, each selecting a choice cigar from the box Farnsworth held out to them.

Pleading weariness, Nell refused Mrs. Selkirk's half-hearted invitation to join her and Miss Benedict for a demitasse of coffee in the drawing room. Her excuse was accepted readily and with ill-concealed relief. Eager to escape, Nell made her way upstairs. The dinner hour had been an ordeal, and she would be glad to reach the peace of her own room.

Nell had always been sensitive and was very much aware of the undercurrents at the Selkirks' dinner table. Clashes of personalities, viewpoints, and attitudes had been extreme. She knew she would need time to sort out the impressions she had received during the evening. Perhaps she could gain perspective by writing some of them in her journal.

*C*oming into her bedroom, Nell was surprised to see that the coverlet had been turned down, her robe and nightgown were laid out on the bed, and her blue embroidered slippers were on the rug beside it. She had not expected maid service. The ambiguity of her position had been clear, and it seemed to make everyone uncomfortable. But then the positions of Miss Benedict and Nanny Maybank were equally confusing: a former children's nurse and a governess, yet both dined with the family. How had Gervase defined it? She must find her own niche, Nell decided, and that depended on Allegra. As Mrs. Russell had pointed out, it was Allegra around whom everything revolved.

Nell took out the journal she had placed in the desk drawer and sat down at the little desk. She dipped her pen in the inkwell, then paused for a minute, pen poised, thinking of the odd assortment of people gathered at dinner, visualizing each face—the wide variety of features, eyes, expressions. Were they all wearing masks? Faces could betray secrets or reveal hidden thoughts. But first impressions could also be misleading.

Nell began to write—short, pithy comments, whatever came into her mind about each individual. Desmond Selkirk, "a domestic despot," his wife, "scared rabbit," Dr. Herbert, "cold, calculating." Miss Benedict? She was a type Nell was familiar with from her job at the inn. Spinsters usually traveling in twos had come on their holidays to the seaside resort. Hard to please, finding fault with the service, the food, their rooms—complaints given in mincing, affected accents. Nell had dealt with them all, maintaining her calm with effort. "Pitiful" was the word that came to mind. Nanny?

What about the old Nanny? Her sudden arrival had caused quite a stir. Still, she seemed to exert some kind of authority over them all in spite of her vague, rather lost behavior. Behind those beady eyes lay—what? Nell spontaneously wrote "wisdom, untold secrets, truth?"

After each name, she wrote "friend or foe?" Nell smiled to herself. Maybe she was letting her pen run amok with fancies. After all, she had been in the Selkirk household less than twenty-four hours. She must keep her traitorous imagination in check.

Aunt Hester had always despaired of what she called Nell's tendency to give ordinary events a more dramatic twist than warranted. Maybe her childish way of making sense out of puzzling situations and mysterious events had somehow carried over into adulthood.

Nell closed her journal and slipped it into the shallow desk drawer. Tomorrow her first meeting with Allegra lay ahead. She wanted so much for it to go well. To get started on the right foot. Allegra's uncle was counting on her making friends with his niece. As she had been taught to do before any new challenging situation, Nell picked up her Bible, trusting that within it she would find some guidance.

For some reason, instead of turning to a familiar psalm or favorite verse, she opened it at random, something Aunt Hester did not condone. Her aunt believed the Bible should be read once through within a year, systematically alternating between the Old and New Testaments. However, this time Nell closed her eyes and let the Bible fall open. Looking down, she saw it was open to Mark 4. Her gaze followed her finger down the lines of print and stopped at verse 22: "For there is nothing hid, which shall not be manifested; neither was any thing kept secret, but that it should come abroad."

Nell read the verse twice. It was almost as if it answered all the questions she had been asking about the strange household into which she had arrived. There was much to discover here. As yet she had no idea of what even tomorrow would bring. Perhaps this was meant to reassure her that everything would eventually be clear. Maybe. At least she supposed that was what she should take from this verse. With a sigh, Nell laid her Bible aside. Suddenly she felt tired, weary from the long day. Everything would seem different in the morning.

A knock on her bedroom door brought Nell fully awake. She hadn't slept well. She had awakened several times during the night, due perhaps to being in a strange bed and unfamiliar surroundings. Sleepily she raised herself on her elbows. A few seconds later, Jewel entered carrying a tray.

"Good mornin', miss. Here's your tea," she said cheerfully, setting the tray on the bedside table.

"You needn't have done that." Nell sat up, pushing the pillows behind her back. "I certainly don't expect you to wait on me."

"I don't see why not, miss." Jewel looked surprised. "I bring up a tray for Miss Benedict. No reason you shouldn't have yours too." She poured a cup of tea and handed it to Nell.

"Still, in the future I can come downstairs for breakfast."

"Nobody but Mr. Selkirk has breakfast downstairs," Jewel said briskly. "Mrs. Selkirk sleeps till eleven and has hers in her room. Wallis, Miss Allegra's personal maid, sees to her whatever time she wakes up."

Jewel paused, as if ready to add something. Then apparently having thought better of it, she said, "I don't think you'd find the master good company if you was to go down. He reads the newspaper all the time he's eatin', then goes through the mornin' mail. Four days a week he goes into the city on business. You might as well enjoy havin' a bit of time to yourself to start off the day right."

Nell sipped her tea and watched Jewel going about the room, pulling back the draperies, checking the towel rack near the washstand. "I'll bring you up some hot water and some clean linens."

Jewel came and stood at the foot of the bed. Nell sensed the girl wanted to say something more but was waiting to be prompted. She suspected the maid was a font of information about the household and all its occupants. However, Nell knew it was not good form to pump servants. She waited, feeling her silence would be encouragement enough if Jewel wanted to talk. She was correct.

"About last night, miss," Jewel said. "In case you was disturbed by Nanny." She took a long breath. "She's a dear old soul, no matter what you might think, and there's nothing wrong with her brain. She mixes up names and dates, forgets things sometimes, but she's sharp as a tack. My own gram was that way too. It's like that with all old folks." Jewel lifted her chin and sniffed. "There's those who'd want to make out like Nanny's daft, but she isn't. Far from it."

Nell nodded. "I understand, Jewel."

Jewel gave her head a little toss. "I jest didn't want you to get the wrong idea."

"That's very kind of you to tell me."

"Well, I best be on my way." Jewel adjusted her ruffled cap more firmly on her head. "Chores don't do themselves." At the door she stopped, then turned back again. "I'm glad you're here to be with Miss Allegra. She needs to have someone young around, not just the—" Jewel halted, as though she decided she ought not say more. "Anyway, we think you'll do her a world of good." With that she went out the door, leaving Nell to wonder who comprised "we."

Nell finished her tea, got up, and dressed. A veil of mystery had begun to surround Nell's image of Allegra, an illusion Nell hoped to push aside to accomplish her mission here.

She had just finished securing her hair into its coil when another rap came at her door.

"I've come to take you to Miss Allegra," Mrs. Russell announced.

"Now?"

"Yes, she just sent word by her maid, Wallis, she wanted to meet you." As if obliged to explain, Mrs. Russell added, "Wallis was also her late mother's personal maid."

Circles within circles, Nell thought. Everything seemed to be connected to everything else and to the past. It was as if the past shadowed everything in this house.

Nell felt nervous. This is what she had come here for; why did she now feel anxiety about this first encounter? She followed Mrs. Russell's statuesque figure down the hall to the suite of rooms in which Allegra had lived for the last year and a half. From what Gervase had told Nell, she had not gone outside the house in all that time. What kept her imprisoned here? This and other thoughts raced through Nell's mind as they neared Allegra's suite.

After Mrs. Russell tapped lightly on the closed door, they waited. From behind it, Nell heard the rustle of skirts and soft footsteps. Someone opened the door slightly, and a face, thin, sallow, and pinched, peered out. The woman looked at Mrs. Russell, then gave Nell a measured glance before stepping back and opening the door for them to pass through into a small, dim entry.

"This is Wallis, Miss Allegra's maid." To the woman she said, "This is Miss Winston. I hope Miss Allegra is well today?"

"As well as can be expected," Wallis replied tersely, nodding at Nell. "She shouldn't stay too long."

"She won't. I'm sure Miss Winston will use discretion." Mrs. Russell seemed to be addressing Nell as well as answering the maid's concern. "I'll leave you now," she said to Nell and left.

Nell was ushered into a room lit only by firelight. Even

though it was ten o'clock in the morning of a bright September day, heavy, velvet curtains were drawn over the windows. She paused on the threshold for a minute to accustom her eyes to the dimness. Then she saw the outline of a figure seated in a deep lounge chair in front of the fireplace. At Nell's approach, the young woman slowly turned her head. The glow from the fire illuminated her face, and Nell saw her at last. Allegra.

Her beauty made Nell draw her breath. It was her eyes that caught first attention. They were huge, velvety brown, dark orbs in the pallor of a heart-shaped face on which only traces of a once healthy complexion remained. Her skin now had the translucence of fine porcelain. Her dark hair fell from a center part in deep waves over either side of her pale face and down over her shoulders. Her mouth was beautifully shaped but drooped at the corners, giving her an expression of sadness.

As Nell moved closer, Allegra seemed to draw back, as if afraid of contact. "Good day, Miss Selkirk; I'm Nell Winston."

Allegra made no reply, and Nell felt rebuffed until she suddenly remembered Gervase had said that Allegra had not spoken since the accident. In nervous reaction, she spoke quickly. "I'm very pleased to meet you at last. Your uncle has spoken so affectionately of you." Nell took a few more steps, extending her hand. Just as she did, a tiny brown and black fur ball leapt up from under the robe covering Allegra's knees and began a cacophony of high-pitched barking. Startled, Nell jumped back, her heart pounding. Then her fright turned to amusement. She saw the source of all the racket—a miniature dog, a Yorkie, his teeth drawn back from a small mouth under a shiny, black nose. He continued to bark and growl, even when his mistress held him close, cuddling him against her. It was so ludicrous—the size of the protective "mastiff" and how much he had scared her, that Nell dissolved into laughter.

"Nasty little beast!" a voice from behind hissed, and with a bustling rustle of taffeta, Clarise Benedict brushed past Nell. Bending over Allegra, her voice changed completely.

"Here, sweetie," she cooed. "Let me take Tippy. Isn't it time Lawrence took him for his walk?"

If Nell had been startled by the fierce little dog's unexpected appearance, she was doubly so at Clarise's. Had she been in the room when Nell came in, or had she slipped in unnoticed, to observe the initial meeting with Allegra? It gave Nell an uncomfortable feeling.

Nell wondered if Allegra had heard Clarise's ill-tempered murmur as she went to remove Tippy. There was a prolonged, affectionate parting before Allegra surrendered the dog. Clarise then motioned Wallis, also standing in the background, to carry the dog away.

Clarise remained for the duration of Nell's visit, a strange visit with no mutual exchange of conversation. Nell tried to tell Allegra a little about herself, but she felt unnaturally stiff knowing that every word and gesture was being monitored by Miss Benedict, who had seated herself in a large chair near them, knitting. Every time Nell happened to glance her way, she was met with a cold stare. Miss Benedict's knitting needles flashed silver in the firelight.

After ten or fifteen minutes, Nell felt this one-sided conversation had gone on long enough. She had also noted Allegra's expression subtly changed from a flicker of interest to indifference and then to a kind of helpless weariness. Conscious that Miss Benedict might be taking some pleasure in the frustration of her futile efforts to elicit some visible response from Allegra, Nell rose reluctantly to leave.

"I don't want to tire you. First meetings are always a little strained. Until one person gets to know another, they search for topics of mutual interest. I hope there will be many such subjects for us. If you enjoy reading, I thought we might read a book together. Perhaps a novel?"

Nell thought she saw a flicker of interest in Allegra's eyes at the mention of this possible pastime.

Just then Miss Benedict bustled over, saying authoritatively, "I think you better go, Miss Winston."

Nell looked at Allegra, who passed a listless hand across her brow and made an attempt at a faint smile.

"I was just leaving, Miss Benedict," Nell replied coolly. To Allegra she said, "Perhaps we could take tea together later?"

"Allegra naps in the afternoon. She doesn't keep regular hours," Miss Benedict interjected now, standing right beside Nell, edging her out. Irritated, Nell ignored her and spoke again to Allegra.

"I want you to know I am happy to conform my time to yours. I look forward to our spending many happy hours together. You have only to send for me." Nell thought she saw some slight encouragement as Allegra nodded and again tried to smile.

The strain of this visit had been quite enough for Nell, as had Allegra's implacable passiveness and Miss Benedict's guardian attitude. With as much poise as she could manage, Nell turned to leave. It was then she saw Wallis, almost obscured by the shadowy light, standing at the door. Silently she opened it, and Nell walked out. Would there always be this wall of protective custody about Allegra?

Back in her room, Nell reviewed the puzzling meeting. In spite of the inhospitable atmosphere in that room, she felt a deep compassion for the young woman. There had been something appealingly childlike about her. Nell recalled as she had been about to leave, Allegra's mouth had moved, quivered nervously, as if she wanted to say something. Had that meant she wanted Nell to stay? Welcomed her offer to be company for her? Had Nell somehow reached her without knowing it?

Instinctively, Nell knew this was a deeply troubled young woman, someone who needed kindness, friendship. Her natural inclination had always been to give help to anyone who needed her. Nell prayed that in spite of the obstacles, even those deliberately put in her way by others, she would become Allegra's friend—if necessary, her defender.

5

*D*ismissed so summarily, told implicitly that Allegra had no need of her company, Nell was left to her own devices for the rest of the day. How was she to spend her time if not in some kind of service to the young woman she'd been hired to companion?

Even on this short acquaintance, Allegra's pitiable condition had touched Nell's sympathetic heart. Beyond the fact that Gervase was paying her, Nell was moved by Allegra's need. How to go about helping the young woman was the question. Several possible ways swirled in Nell's thoughts. She should put them in some sort of order; she could experiment with one thing, and if that didn't work, try something else. First, she must determine how to get through the wall of resistance that both Miss Benedict and Wallis formed around Allegra.

She walked over to the window and looked out. From this side of the house, Nell could view the garden, the sloping terrace that led through a small copse of willows down to the lake at the end of the property. Suddenly, she felt a yearning to be outside in the early autumn sunshine, away from the gloomy interior of the house. She had always found walking a good antidote to muddled thoughts, and there was no reason to believe it would not work in this case.

She descended the staircase and, once downstairs, went through the foyer, past the library and the morning room to the glassed conservatory at the far end. Off this was a small tiled cloakroom leading through French doors to the garden. Beside it stood a hall tree on which hung a tweed ulster and an assortment of broad-brimmed hats; underneath lay a clutter of Wellingtons and rubber boots.

Outside, Nell took a long breath of the fresh, damp air. She started walking, thinking of the problem facing her. First, she had to win Allegra's trust, get to know her; she would have to find out what Allegra cared about most.

Deep in thought, Nell sauntered past the hedged entrance to the beautifully designed garden. Curved gravel paths meandered through intricately shaped flower beds. Now, in fall, only a few flowers were in bloom: bronze and gold chrysanthemums, purple cosmos, russet and yellow marigolds. Still, they were a lovely sight and a nice contrast to the somber gray stone house looming over them.

As she strolled along the winding paths, Nell spotted whimsical touches. Here and there were small statuary: figures of children rolling hoops, dancing, holding hands in a circle, bending to touch a flower or examine a small stone frog. Sculptures of tiny woodland creatures—bunnies, squirrels—appeared unexpectedly under flowering bushes or nestled half hidden under hawthorne hedges. In the center was a circular brick fishpond with water lilies. Nell stopped to watch as goldfish, flashes of brilliant light, swam in their underwater ballet. In nooks sheltered by espaliered fruit trees were wrought iron benches where a wanderer could sit and quietly meditate or simply enjoy the loveliness of the garden.

The garden must have been someone's joy. Perhaps it had been Allegra's mother's. Or maybe it was a pleasure the happy couple had shared. Unlike the house, where only a few remnants of the happiness it once held lingered, this garden remained a lasting symbol of the magical childhood Allegra must have enjoyed with her beloved parents.

Nell left the garden and followed the stepping stones down the terrace leading to the lake. A long wood dock stretched out into the water. There was a small boathouse to the left but no boats in sight.

She walked to the end of the dock where there was a sign on one of the posts. Washed away by wind, rain, and age, the letters on the weathered board were almost illegible. The first word was HOPE'S, but most of the second word was missing. Only two letters remained entirely visible, the N and D. Nell sounded out what it must have read when newly painted, "Hope's Landing." So that had been the original name of the Selkirk estate . . . not "Hope's End." Strange that the name by which it was now known was more accurate than the first.

The wind rose, sending ripples across the smooth surface of the lake, and Nell shivered. She turned and started back toward the house. She looked up at its stone facade. In the slanted light the windows seemed blank. What lay behind each one was a mystery.

It was hard to believe that the house had once held love, laughter, and life for a loving husband and wife and their daughter. But it must have. From what Gervase Montgomery had told Nell, his sister and brother-in-law had been vivacious people, fond of entertaining, enjoying each other to the fullest. An ideal happily married couple. Made for each other. Gervase had said, "With them it had been love at first sight, and that love never wavered but grew stronger and deeper each year. It was fulfilled by the birth of Allegra. I've never known a more loving trio." Gervase's eyes had darkened with pain at the memory of what had been so cruelly lost.

Nell suppressed a shudder. Not yet ready to return to the dreary house, she turned at a cross path and took another direction. This path led to the stables. Coming closer, she saw a well-kept stone building with white painted paddocks and a large cobblestone courtyard. There were two young boys, grooms probably, busily at work, one mucking out stalls at the lower end, the other rubbing down a beautiful roan-colored horse.

As she approached, a man emerged from the side of what was possibly the tack room. Hugh Douglass. He seemed about to give an order to one of the grooms when he saw her and stopped. He looked surprised; taking a few long strides toward her, he removed his cap and said, "Good day, miss." There was inquiry in his voice, and again she caught a hint of a Scottish burr.

"Good day, Mr. Douglass. I'm out exploring. I've been through the garden and down to the lake. What a wonderful place this is."

"Yes," he said, nodding. "Too bad it's so little enjoyed or appreciated. It wasn't always that way. When the other Mr. Selkirk was alive and—" he halted abruptly as if he'd said too much.

Nell studied him more consciously than she had the previous day. Then she had been too self-concerned to notice anything other than his strong features and how handsome he was. There was something else arresting about him. Nell did not quite know what—something melancholy in his expression, as if he carried some unknown burden.

Her wandering thoughts were jolted back to the moment by his question. "Do you ride, miss?"

"No, I'm afraid not." Nell shook her head regretfully. "I never had the opportunity to learn."

"Too bad. Miss Allegra's horse, Princess, could use a lady rider. She's gentle and has a sweet mouth."

"Is that Princess?" Nell asked, pointing to the sleek horse one of the stable hands was grooming.

"Yes, come take a look," Hugh suggested, and he led the way over to her. "If you did ride, it would be a great help. She's a fine little horse but not properly exercised. I have one of the grooms take her out as often as I can spare him. But it's not enough. She used to be ridden every day. Miss Allegra never missed a day before the accident." A look of genuine sadness crossed Hugh Douglass's face. "It's a real shame. Mr. Selkirk—Desmond, that is—says he's going to sell her unless Miss Allegra recovers, and from what I hear there's not much possibility of that."

"But there's always hope," Nell said impulsively.

Hugh looked skeptical. "Not likely, I gather. Not unless you believe in fairy tales and magic potions, or—" he gave a short laugh, "—miracles."

"Miracles I do believe in," Nell retorted staunchly, not adding she intended to be part of one.

Hugh threw her another look she couldn't quite interpret then put his hand on Princess's halter and led her back into one of the stalls. He closed the gate and went to the next stall. This time he brought out a golden-maned mare who tossed her head, whinnying.

"Now this one's another story." Hugh grinned and rubbed the arched neck affectionately. "Wild and stubborn but a great spirit. I have to ride Sheherazade daily or there'd be no riding her at all."

Nell wondered why Hugh Douglass made sure this horse was exercised regularly and not Allegra's. Had he given up on Princess's owner, lost hope? It was Nell's understanding that everything, the house, the stables, all the horses, belonged to Allegra. Gervase had told her Allegra had inherited her parents' fortune.

His next words gave her a clue. "Funny how horses reflect their owners. One can be as mild and placid as a Milquetoast. Others need a tight rein, need to be shown who's in charge. This is Miss Felicity's horse. She brought it with her when she moved here after the accident. Didn't want to leave it when they shipped her off to her fancy boarding school." A muscle in his cheek flexed, and his mouth pressed into a line. "She's a daring rider. Takes the fences and walls and is off onto the moors like an Arabian." He smiled as if seeing this in his mind's eye and relishing the scene he was describing. "And Sheherazade reacts to that. She's always raring to go even when I ride her. But soon she'll be ridden to her heart's desire. Everything will be all right when Miss Felicity comes."

Why, he's in love with her, Nell thought. He spoke of the horse and Felicity as if they were one. She watched as he stroked the golden velvet nose and spoke to Sheherazade softly as he dug into his jacket pocket for sugar lumps. He fed her from his palm, his hand caressing her gently. Yes, that was it. Hugh Douglass was taking special care of this horse for one reason. He was in love with its mistress.

"Then it will be different when Miss Felicity comes home?" Nell asked, observing Hugh closely.

"Ah, indeed, it will. Everything will be different then."

Nell said good-bye and started back to the house. She stopped once and looked back just in time to see Hugh saddling Sheherazade, preparing to take her out for a ride.

As she walked along slowly, Nell wondered if the Selkirks had any idea their stable master was in love with their daughter. More interesting to know, was that love mutual?

6

*U*pon nearing the house, Nell heard the sound of wild barking. Unmistakably it was Allegra's Yorkie. Just ahead, she saw the footman, Lawrence, to whose unfortunate lot walking the little dog must have fallen, pulling the protesting Tippy along the path. The footman was tugging the leash and accompanying his effort by some uninhibited swearing.

Quickening her pace, Nell called, "Wait, Lawrence."

He stopped and turned; when he realized Nell had been within earshot, he turned beet red. "Sorry, miss, but this dratted little dog—" he halted, flustered. Tippy was spinning around on his back legs, twisting the leash Lawrence was jerking until man and dog were hopelessly entangled.

"'e's impossible, miss," the entrapped footman grumbled over the frantic barking. "It's more'n a body can manage to walk 'im proper. 'e sat down most of the way; had to be dragged, 'e did—"

"Wait a minute; let me see if I can help," Nell offered. She bent down and captured the wiggling little body in both hands. The animal was quivering, but, at her touch, his yipping subsided a little. She moved her fingers in his soft fur

and gently kneaded the dog's neck, speaking in a low, sooth-
ing tone, "There, there, it's all right." She wrapped both arms
around him, cradling him against her breast.

"Well, I say, miss. You seem to have a way with 'im. I'll be
dashed if I do," Lawrence said in an awed tone. "I never seen
nobody but Miss Allegra herself who could get 'im calmed
down like that."

At his words, an idea struck Nell. Maybe this was an answer to her prayer for insight on how she could help Allegra.
Obviously, she adored her little pet. He was her comfort, her
security, probably the only link to her happy past. Perhaps
the Yorkie had been a gift from her parents on some special
occasion. What if Nell would offer to take on the duty of walking Tippy every day? It might be the key to getting close to
Allegra, gaining her confidence, her trust.

Yes, it might work. Maybe this incident had given her the
clue for which she had been searching. Still holding Tippy,
Nell stood up.

"I'll take him back up to Miss Allegra."

"All right, miss." Lawrence nodded, visibly relieved.

They walked the rest of the way back to the house together,
Nell carrying Tippy. When they reached the entrance to the
cloakroom Lawrence hesitated, then said awkwardly, "I'm
sure glad you came by when you did, miss. I'd be grateful if
you wasn't to mention this here little fracas we've had . . . I'm
not used to dogs like this one. On me dad's farm we've got
all sorts of animals—dogs and all. I was brought up that you
had to be the master; command them and they learned to
obey or else get a good whuppin'." He paused, still looking
flushed and embarrassed. "But it wouldn't be worth my job
here if anyone was to lay a hand on that one." He gave Tippy
an accusing look. The dog just whined softly, burrowed
deeper into Nell's arms.

"It's all right, Lawrence. I won't say anything to Miss
Allegra."

"Nor to Wallis either, please, ma'am. It's 'er that would

rouse a fuss," Lawrence continued. He turned and hung up the tweed ulster on the hook of the coatrack. "I don't want no trouble with 'er nor Miss Benedict either." His voice had a pleading note.

"It's not necessary for anyone to know, Lawrence. Dogs are like people in some ways. They take to certain ones for no real reason and to others, they don't," Nell said tactfully. She understood this big, raw-boned farm boy probably had only recently gone into service and had not a glimmer of how to treat a pampered lapdog. "Don't worry. I'll take care of it. I'll ask Miss Allegra if I can walk Tippy from now on."

"Thank you, miss," Lawrence said, gratitude written all over his face.

Nell carried Tippy through the hall to the foot of the staircase, then set him down and unsnapped the leash from his collar. Quick as a dart, he scampered ahead of her up the steps so fast she was hard put to keep up with him. He flew down the corridor and was scratching at Allegra's door by the time Nell reached it.

The door was opened by Wallis, who gave Nell a puzzled frown. Tippy raced over to Allegra's chair and leapt up, with ecstatic whimperings, onto her lap. Allegra cuddled the little dog as if the two had been separated for longer than a mere thirty minutes. Over his head, her large dark eyes met Nell's questioningly.

Ignoring Wallis, who had positioned herself in the doorway, Nell walked over to Allegra.

"Would it be all right with you if from now on I took Tippy out for his walk every day? I'm quite fond of dogs, and I enjoy getting out myself for fresh air and exercise. It would be no trouble for me at all."

Allegra's thin, pale hand fondled the little dog's ears, and he responded by kissing her cheek with his small pink tongue. It was then that Nell first saw a trace of a smile appear on Allegra's face. That tentative smile was a confirmation of Nell's idea—that the way to Allegra's heart might be through her little dog.

Allegra nodded agreement, and Nell left, satisfied that she had accomplished a small victory.

After that, Nell came to get Tippy every day. The little dog adapted to the new routine, and his plumy tail even wagged a bit in anticipation when Nell appeared and rattled his leash.

Although nobody else wanted the chore, Nell sensed some resentment in both Wallis and Miss Benedict when she arrived in Allegra's room to pick up her charge.

Not that they were doing anything to cheer Allegra up or engage her in any kind of activity, a card game or needlework, or any such pastime an invalid might enjoy. Nell was disturbed to find that Allegra was usually sitting in her darkened room, staring blankly into space. It was neither good nor healthy. Nell fumed. The young woman was retreating more and more into some kind of dangerous space, far from reality. Didn't anyone else see that? Wasn't anyone else trying to bring her out of it?

After dinner on the first Saturday evening Nell was at Hope's End, Mrs. Selkirk announced that a group would be going to church in the morning. "We attend Grace Chapel in the village. You are welcome to go with us—that is—" she hesitated, "unless—" she paused, "that is, if you're not a dissenter?"

Nell suppressed a smile, wondering if she should present her baptismal and confirmation certificate for validation. "No, I'm Church of England, Mrs. Selkirk," she replied demurely.

"Ah, well, then," said Mrs. Selkirk, relieved, "we leave the house at half past ten—in time for the eleven o'clock service."

Feeling in need of divine assistance in her new challenge, Nell was eager to see if the service at the village church would bestow some of its name upon her. Grace was what she needed, along with discernment, long-suffering, and kindness.

The next morning, dressed in her checked coat with its velvet collar and cuffs and her best black velvet bonnet with the plum-colored ribbons, Nell went downstairs promptly at half past ten and was waiting when Mrs. Selkirk, Miss Benedict, and Mrs. Russell descended the stairway. Nell hadn't counted on Clarise's company, but she and Mrs. Selkirk seemed on friendly terms, and in the carriage they carried on a conversation all the way to church. Mrs. Russell read her small prayer book, Nell supposed to avoid the trivial chitchat of the other two. Mr. Selkirk, silent, grim, evidently an unwilling attendee, sat morosely staring out the window on the trip.

As far as an inspiring sermon was concerned, Nell was disappointed, but the familiar liturgy, Scripture readings, and Eucharist were all comforting. The vicar was an elderly man and probably repeated his homilies year after year, simply bringing them out on the appropriate Sundays.

After the service, they all filed outside where members of the congregation assembled in small groups, chatting. It was then Nell first noticed the man with a lean, interesting face and serious expression regarding her with thoughtful eyes, almost as if he knew her. He was a short distance away from the Selkirk group, standing beside another young man who bore a strong resemblance to him. Not wanting to stare, Nell turned away. But even her casual glance registered the fact that both were extremely good-looking, dressed splendidly in clothes that were obviously London tailored.

Nell had had enough experience at the Seaview Inn to be able to tell a gentleman when she saw one. These two were certainly that. She was surprised when she saw the two approach Mr. Selkirk, who greeted them heartily.

"Well, the Lewis brothers! Good to see you, Hamilton." He addressed the taller one, the one who had been looking at Nell. "And you too, Thomas, my boy. Down from Oxford, are you?"

They conversed for a few minutes until Mrs. Selkirk, who had been chatting with another lady, joined them. Nell was standing close enough to hear the exchange between them.

The younger man asked, "And when will Miss Felicity be home, sir?"

Mr. Selkirk mumbled something in his gruff way, but at that point Mrs. Selkirk finished whatever she was saying and moved to her husband's side, greeting the two men effusively.

"Thomas, Hamilton, how nice to see you both. Down for the weekend, or are you staying?"

"Just for a few days, ma'am, but Mother will be opening the house for the holidays," the man she had addressed as Hamilton replied. The other, Thomas, chimed in enthusiastically, "We're looking forward to that, Mrs. Selkirk. There will be lots of parties and festivities; I do hope Miss Felicity will be here to enjoy them." His eyes were shining, his smile eager. *Aha,* Nell thought. *Miss Felicity definitely has an admirer.*

"Indeed, she will. And we are planning a party of our own to which you are both invited," Mrs. Selkirk said, then wagged a finger playfully at the older brother. "That means you too, Hamilton; although I know you avoid most social events. Your mother told me so to her despair!"

"It would be our pleasure." Hamilton smiled, and, over her shoulder, his gaze rested on Nell to whom he nodded. Then he turned toward her, remarking to Mrs. Selkirk, "I haven't had the honor of meeting your guest yet."

"My guest?" Mrs. Selkirk sounded bewildered. "What guest?"

Hamilton bowed slightly and looked directly at Nell.

"This young lady." His smile transformed his face entirely.

Wide-eyed and surprised, Mrs. Selkirk looked around, then seeing Nell, stammered, "She's not my guest—she's Allegra's—well, I suppose you'd say her companion."

Ignoring Mrs. Selkirk's floundering, Hamilton continued to regard Nell with interest.

Finally, Mrs. Selkirk got out her name, "Miss Nell Winston, Mr. Hamilton Lewis."

"Delighted," he said, the smile widening.

Nell felt embarrassed at the awkward introduction. She

felt the color flood into her face. How humiliating to be passed over then reluctantly introduced as if she had no social position.

It brought back another experience that she had thrust deep into her memory, that still hurt too much think about. That memory made her stiff and cold with remembered shame, and she only inclined her head slightly as Hamilton Lewis stepped over to start a conversation.

His attempt was abruptly cut short, for at that moment, the Selkirks' carriage drew up, and Mr. Selkirk, anxious to get home to his port and the London paper, herded his entourage together to depart. Mrs. Russell finished her chat with the vicar, and Clarise reluctantly withdrew from her conversation with Dr. Herbert and came over to the carriage where Lawrence held the door open. He assisted the ladies inside while Mr. Selkirk said good-bye to the Lewis brothers.

As soon as they got back, Nell went straight upstairs to her room. She wished the uncomfortable meeting with the Lewises hadn't taken place. She was flooded with the memory of one of the unhappiest times in her life. A time she had tried hard to forget.

At age sixteen, Nell had been invited home by her roommate, Jennifer Mobray, for a spring house party at her family's country estate, Henley Hall. In the small school the aunts ran, there were only twenty-eight girls. Jennifer and Nell had paired off at once and were each other's special friend. Jennifer's parents had sent their carriage for them, and Nell remembered how thrilled she had been. All the way to the Mobray home, the two girls had chatted and giggled excitedly, planning the holiday ahead.

"My brother Dennis is bringing some of his friends from school, and Mama is giving us a dancing party with a midnight buffet supper," Jennifer told Nell.

Henley Hall was grander than any house Nell had ever seen. Its manicured lawns were vast, and the house itself was huge, elegantly furnished. The girls had adjoining rooms in one wing. The Mobrays had welcomed Nell, and she anticipated a wonderful time. And then Dennis and his friends had arrived from their school.

Almost from the beginning, Nell had been attracted to Jennifer's handsome brother, and, by the first evening, it was evident the attraction was mutual. Dennis was blessed with good looks, good nature, good humor. Whether he was aware of it or not, he also had a natural irresistible charm and knew how to use it.

By the second evening, he and Nell danced with no one else, conversed exclusively, walked together, chose each other as partners in a variety of parlor games, sought each other out on all possible occasions. It was after the fourth evening, the night of the dance and supper party Mrs. Mobray had given, that the blow fell.

The following morning, when the maid brought Nell her tea tray, she roused her from a sound sleep, telling her that Mrs. Mobray wanted to see her in the morning room as soon as she was dressed. Since it was very early and they had all gone to bed only a few hours before, Nell, sleepy-eyed and confused, did as directed. When she entered the morning room, she faced a cool reception. Gone was the gracious hostess who had greeted her warmly upon arrival; in her place was a cold-eyed stranger.

In a few words, Mrs. Mobray conveyed the fact that Nell was to leave at once, that the maid was packing her things. "This may be hard for you to understand now, but later on you will. We have plans for Dennis that do not include infatuation with girls not of his class. He is a headstrong, impetuous boy, and, from what I've observed over the last few days, his heart may rule his head. As parents, we have to guide and protect our son so that he will neither make some youthful mistake that will ruin his life nor make any romantic promises that would break your heart."

Nell had stood, stunned, bewildered as Mrs. Mobray said

all this. She could hardly believe what she was hearing. Of course, she and Dennis had danced, laughed, and delighted in each other's company, and, yes, there had been a few stolen kisses as they strolled in the garden and behind the exotic tropical palm in the glass conservatory off the ballroom . . . but they had never spoken of love or any future commitment.

But Mrs. Mobray gave her no time to explain or make excuses. She had simply stood up, bringing the discussion to an end, and opened the door into the hall for Nell. There Nell saw her bags neatly lined up by the front door. Outside, the carriage was waiting. She turned to ask Mrs. Mobray if she might say good-bye to Jennifer, but already the morning room door was closing.

Humiliated, heartbroken, Nell had been taken back to her aunts a full week before she was expected. She mumbled an explanation that she was probably coming down with a cold. Her swollen eyes and red nose gave enough evidence of that possibility to be believed. Sympathetically, she was tucked into her bed, piled with quilts by the concerned aunts, given a flannel-wrapped warm brick at her feet, brought a hot lemon tea, and left to recover.

The experience might have eventually lost its sting for Nell if it had not had unexpected repercussions. At holiday's end, Jennifer did not return to the Miss Winstons' Academy for Young Ladies. A letter was received from Jennifer's mother that the Mobrays had made other arrangements for their daughter's education. The financial loss of her tuition fees for a half a year dented the aunts' income considerably. Nell felt miserably guilty to be the cause. And yet she could not bring herself to tell them what had really happened.

It was not until much later that Nell was able to look at that painful episode and see it for what it was. Mrs. Mobray's action had been an example of class discrimination at its worst. Because Nell wasn't from a family of wealth and prestige, she was not deemed suitable for their son. The fact that

Nell and Dennis had enjoyed each other in all innocence without a thought of the future was irrelevant.

What hurt most was the loss of Jennifer's friendship. Nell couldn't believe her dearest friend and confidante could share her snobbish mother's opinion. But when Nell tried writing to Jennifer at Henley Hall, her letters were returned unopened.

It was a bitter lesson, and one Nell had learned well. She made a decision then that she would guard her heart and never, never open it recklessly to anyone above her social station.

8

*T*he next day Nell decided to go into the village, where she hoped to purchase an interesting book, a puzzle, or maybe a board game that would bring some variety to Allegra's days. She also needed to go to the post office.

Over the weekend she had written a letter to Gervase Montgomery, telling him she had arrived at Hope's End and had begun her duties as his niece's companion. She had hesitated to be too explicit about the dismaying situation she had discovered. However, he was trusting her to be honest, to send him her observations. His parting words to her had been that he was depending on her integrity. After a few false starts, she had finally completed a brief but guarded account of her assessment of Allegra's condition. She finished with, "She needs more mental stimulation—something to bring her out of herself and involve her in the outside world. This I shall try to accomplish."

After rereading the letter, she sealed the envelope and addressed it to Mr. Montgomery's London club. Then she put on her jacket, hat, and sturdy boots and left for the village.

The village was small, consisting of one winding street. At one end was The Red Fox Inn and at the far end the train station. In between there was a greengrocery, a fabric store, a pub called The White Knight, and a variety of other small shops. Nell decided to go first to the post office to purchase some stamps and mail her letter. Then she would explore the shops.

The post office was crowded, and Nell had to wait in line to be helped. When she reached the counter, a wiry middle-aged woman with carrot-red hair swirled up in a corkscrew bun cocked her head and looked at Nell with bright blue, inquisitive eyes. "What can I do for you, miss?"

"I'd like some postage stamps, please."

"How many?"

Nell told her the amount, and after the woman had counted out the stamps and pushed them over the counter to Nell, she said, "I'm Mrs. Pulham. You're staying up at the Selkirks' place, right?"

Nell shouldn't have been surprised at the question, given the size of the village. Everything that went on in a small town was grist for the gossip mill.

"Yes. I'm Nell Winston, Miss Allegra's companion," Nell said, assuming the woman probably knew that already.

"Poor lass," the postmistress said. "She used to be down here near every day . . . would poke her pretty head in the door even if she didn't want to buy stamps or pick up her letters, just to say hello. A sweet thing she was. She'd ride in on that horse of hers, jump down—a picture in her bright green riding dress." The woman made a clucking sound with her tongue, indicating, Nell guessed, her regret over what had happened to Allegra. "And her parents . . . a nicer couple you'd never meet. Real handsome pair they were too." She gave Nell a sharp glance. "I guess you didn't know them?" Her eyebrows raised as she took the coins Nell gave her, counting them out. "Well, as I always say, one don't know from one day to the next what's in store. And that's the truth."

Since others were lining up behind her and the woman directly in back of her had an armful of packages, Nell nodded and said good-bye. She put her letter to Gervase in the London slot and left the post office.

She crossed the street and walked slowly up the other side until she saw a sign for a stationer's. Since she had not spotted a bookstore, she thought this would be the most likely place to buy a book.

The storekeeper, a gray-haired man with spectacles, looked up as she entered and greeted her with a friendly smile. "Good day, miss. Anything I can help you with today?"

"Do you sell books?" she asked.

"A few. We don't keep a large stock. Most folks around here order from the London stores, so I have only the most popular titles. Dickens, of course. They're all on the shelves over there." He gestured to the back of the store.

Nell thanked him and began walking toward the section he had indicated, pausing along the way to look at other items. There were art supplies: watercolors, brushes, and instruction books. *Would Allegra be interested in painting?* Nell wondered. While she lingered at the display, she happened to look out the store window and saw a man dismounting from a fine-looking horse in front of the store.

Hamilton Lewis! And he was coming into the stationer's. Involuntarily, Nell stepped back. Unreasonably, her heart quickened. Of all people she hadn't expected to see, didn't want to see, it was Hamilton Lewis. The awkward incident outside church on Sunday came back to her. Of course, it had not been his fault; still, the memory made her feel unsettled.

She looked around for a place to escape, but there was nowhere in such a small shop. She knew she must speak if he saw her, recognized or, indeed, even remembered her.

The bell over the store door jangled, and he came inside. He and the storekeeper exchanged hearty greetings.

"Mr. Lewis."

"Good day, Mr. Ives. I've come to pick up the mono-grammed writing paper my mother ordered."

"Of course. It came back from the engraver's this morning. It's in the storeroom. I'll fetch it right away. I hope Lady Anne will be pleased with the way it turned out."

Lady Anne! Nell noted. So Hamilton's mother was of the nobility. That put him even further out of her reach socially.

She moved unobtrusively toward the bookshelves, hoping she would not catch Hamilton's attention. But her move was in vain. While waiting for the clerk to return with his mother's stationery, Hamilton sauntered casually around the shop. Then he saw her.

"Why, Miss Winston. What a nice surprise." Immediately he came over to her.

"Mr. Lewis." Nell kept her response polite but distant. She did not want to betray how much the fact that he had remembered her name pleased her.

Hamilton Lewis was the epitome of everything attractive but dangerous. She admired the courteous manners, the casual charm men of his class seemed to exhibit so easily. These qualities were inbred. Hamilton was also extraordinarily handsome, tall, and broad shouldered. He looked especially fit in his country tweeds. Now, as he stood only a few feet away, she noticed his wavy, chestnut hair and noble features. Finding his nearness unsettling, she took a few steps away and began examining the books.

"Are you a reader, Miss Winston?" Hamilton asked, following her. "Are you looking for a special book?" he asked as her hand drew one out. Truthfully, she hadn't noticed which one until Hamilton went on, "*David Copperfield,* a great choice. I'm not sure which one I like better, that one or *A Tale of Two Cities.* Perhaps the latter since it poses such a profound question. Sidney Carlton's courage has always astounded me. To give up one's life for a loved one—I don't know." Hamilton shook his head, smiling ruefully.

"That is one of my favorites too," Nell said impulsively. Then, in case it sounded as if she were agreeing only for effect, she quickly said, "Actually, I'm looking for something for Allegra. And I suppose it should be something less dark."

"How is Miss Allegra? No one has seen her for months, of course, since the accident. But I remember her well. I'd often see her galloping full-gait on her horse, hair flying, looking as though she were having the time of her life. I was very sorry to hear of her problems. We were all glad to know she was going to have a young companion. I'm sure it's done her a great deal of good."

"You're very kind to say so," Nell said, touched by the sincerity of his concern. "I trust it has. I don't know . . ." she hesitated. "I've been thinking that perhaps I should search for something to stimulate her imagination, get her to take more interest in life." Nell halted, wondering if she was saying too much. But Hamilton was listening intently, as if taking her quest seriously.

"I know what you mean. Confinement and lack of physical activity tend to dull the brain as well as the body. I'm aware of this, because my father had a hunting accident last fall. Thrown by his horse shying at a fence. One leg was badly injured, and he was laid up for months. My mother nearly went mad trying to find things to entertain him." Hamilton smiled as if in rueful retrospect. "Maybe a game of some kind, something to sharpen the wits?"

"Yes, that's what I was thinking. But I didn't know what kind."

"How about cribbage? It's easy enough to learn and quite challenging. I think they have them here." Hamilton glanced around the store, then saw a sign on which was printed Parlor Pastimes. "Let's look over here," Hamilton suggested, leading the way.

In no time, a cribbage board was found, including the instructions; next a deck of playing cards was needed. "That should do it," Hamilton said, triumphantly carrying everything to the counter. Hamilton's package was wrapped, and Mr. Ives was waiting at the counter. He beamed as he wrapped up Nell's purchases.

Nell and Hamilton started out of the store together. Outside, he asked, "Now that we've both completed our errands, would you do me the honor of having tea with me? There's a nice little tea shop down the street."

Nell could easily have been persuaded to accept. She was grateful for his help in selecting the game for Allegra. It would have been most enjoyable to have tea with this charming, intelligent man. Especially after her weeks of isolation and exclusion from congenial company. She was also flattered by the invitation.

But the memory of the past plus her newly acquired knowledge of his titled background sent warning signals. Why set herself up for another crushing snub? Perhaps Hamilton Lewis was under the mistaken impression that she was some kin to Allegra. A poor relation, possibly, to take the position of companion. But even a distant relative could claim some status to landed gentry such as the Selkirks. Whatever he thought, Nell decided it was best not to tempt fate.

So she checked her own inclination and instead said, "Thank you, but I must get back to Allegra. It is our habit to have tea together."

An expression of genuine disappointment came over his face. "Another time, perhaps?"

Nell didn't reply, just smiled.

"I hope Miss Allegra enjoys playing cribbage. Do let me know. If not, maybe we can select something else for her," he said as he walked alongside Nell to the end of the lane. "I would offer you a ride back to the Selkirks' but I've come on horseback as you see."

"I like walking."

"I suppose you don't have much free time?" He made the statement more like a question.

She looked at him, surprised by his persistence. Where was it leading? Maybe Hamilton was at loose ends, down in the country at this particular time, between summer and the beginning of the winter holiday season. Looking for amusement, some female companionship? She couldn't guess his motives. Whatever they were, for her own sake, she knew she must discourage him. She could only guess the pitfalls of encouraging a relationship with the son of Lady Anne.

"My time is more or less at Allegra's disposal; I try to be available for her."

"We have a wonderful library at home. My mother is a voracious reader, loves to talk about books as well as share them. Perhaps she could suggest a suitable book Miss Allegra might enjoy. Besides," Hamilton added almost shyly, "I'm sure she would like to meet you as well . . . if that could be arranged."

Nell felt her cheeks warm under his gaze. She kept her voice steadier than her heart as she replied demurely, "Thank you, but I cannot make any plans of my own at present. Now, you'll have to excuse me, Mr. Lewis. I don't want to keep Allegra waiting."

"Of course; I shan't delay you longer. It was very nice to see you again, Miss Winston. Good day."

"Good day, Mr. Lewis, and thank you again for your help." Nell turned to take the road that led back to Hope's End. Although she didn't look back, she had the distinct feeling that Hamilton Lewis's eyes were following her.

September 25, 1893

I have been at Hope's End a little less than a month. I believe I have made some progress in what Gervase Montgomery hired me to do. The schedule of my days and my time with Allegra have now been established. Mornings are pretty much my own. I write letters, sew or read, walk to the village or down to the lake. After lunch, I go to Allegra's room and we have our reading session, which I think is going well. Then I take Tippy for his outing while Allegra naps. We have tea together at four and sometimes, if she is not too tired, she asks me to have supper on a tray with her, and we continue reading into the early evening. I still feel the hostility of Miss Benedict and Wallis at the amount of time I spend with Allegra. Why? I cannot understand. One would think anyone who cared for Allegra would be happy to see her enjoying herself, having new interests. But I have met opposition in almost everything I have tried to initiate.

Nell paused in her writing. She recalled two recent encounters that left her baffled.

The first day Nell brought *David Copperfield* to show Allegra, upon seeing the title, Miss Benedict said disdainfully, "Dickens? I find him coarse and disgustingly sentimental."

But Allegra herself was eager to begin.

A couple days later, Miss Benedict confronted Nell in the hall. "Do you really think Dickens is the right selection for reading to an invalid? Why not something more cheerful, something by Jane Austen perhaps?"

"Allegra is enjoying this very much. She told me Dickens is one of her favorite authors," Nell replied mildly.

Miss Benedict tossed her head indignantly and walked away.

Nell was too astonished to utter a word in her own defense. Her impression of Allegra's enjoyment of the story had been entirely different. Allegra seemed to look forward to each day's chapter, and her written notes were more and more specific. Their written discussions were interesting and began to tell Nell much about the young woman.

One afternoon, after finishing the chapter in which David safely reaches his aunt Betsy Trotwood's house, Allegra wrote, "How wonderful that an orphan like David found a loving relative to go to who cared so much for him."

"You have such a relative, Allegra," Nell said gently. "Your uncle Gervase is extremely fond of you and cares deeply about you."

Allegra's expression became pensive. Her pencil hesitated above the pad she held, then she wrote something and handed it to Nell to read.

"Uncle Gervase? He hasn't come to see me in weeks. He hasn't written."

Nell read the words in disbelief. That didn't sound right. If Allegra had seen the distress in Gervase Montgomery's eyes, heard the earnestness of his voice when he spoke about her, she would have to know how concerned he was, how anxious to help her recover. That is, unless Nell had been very mistaken about him.

She looked at Allegra and wondered if she should tell her about her surprise meeting with Mr. Montgomery and divulge what he had said about Desmond forbidding him to come here. Didn't she know her two uncles were in strong disagreement about her treatment? Was this one of those areas only a fool would trespass? Family affairs were always treacherous waters for the outsider. Wasn't that what Dr. Herbert had implied in his talk with her?

Carefully, Nell suggested, "Have you thought that you might write to him? Tell him you miss him, let him know how you are?"

Allegra looked thoughtful, then wrote, "Perhaps."

Nell left it at that and went on to other things. But that night, in her room, she wondered if she should write another letter to Gervase, let him know that his niece felt he had deserted her.

As the reading went on, Nell felt gratified that she and Allegra were growing closer through these shared times. Nell knew it was important to earn her trust, and she was becoming genuinely fond of Allegra. She still had to meet the combined hostility of Miss Benedict and Wallis though.

Wallis always acted as though Nell's arrival interrupted something, threw off her schedule. Great sighs, rolling of eyes, pursed mouth were the usual signs of her irritation. Miss Benedict's attitude was even more overt. She made a great show of thrusting her knitting needles viciously into her bag, then, head averted, sweeping past Nell out of the room. Nell tried to ignore it all. It was worse when Miss Benedict stayed in the room during the reading session, making her disapproval apparent.

Nell's reading *David Copperfield* to Allegra continued until one day something unaccountable happened. They had come to the chapter about Dora's death, and as Nell glanced up from the page, she saw tears sliding down Allegra's face. Evidently Miss Benedict saw them too, because she thrust her knitting aside and rushed to Allegra's side. Taking her hand, she stroked it, then gave Nell a pointed look. "That's enough reading for today, Miss Winston. Can't you see this is too much for Miss Allegra?"

Contrite, Nell closed the book and stood up. "I'm sorry. I didn't—"

She was cut off as Wallis pushed past her, making clucking noises. Hurriedly, she soaked a linen handkerchief with cologne and dabbed Allegra's forehead.

Feeling she was in the way, Nell murmured, "I'll be back later to take Tippy out for his walk," and left the room feeling admonished by the other two women.

Afterwards, alone in her room, Nell wondered if she had been at fault. Was she to blame? Had she made the wrong choice of book as Miss Benedict declared? Of course, Dickens was notorious for wringing every possible tear from such scenes in his novels. That is why some criticized his work as overemotional. But it was also why people loved his stories. It gave them a chance to weep, vent some of their own personal sadness. In a way, it was probably a good thing for Allegra to cry a little. She was almost too stoic. She seemed to keep her true feelings locked in.

Nell hoped Allegra would be feeling better when she went to pick up Tippy. However, when Nell went to Allegra's room, she was met by Wallis, her mouth grimly set, who told her, "Miss Allegra is sleeping. She had a headache, and Miss Benedict gave her some laudanum to sleep. It's the only thing that helps when she has one of her headaches." Wallis folded her arms in front of her, anchoring herself firmly in the doorway.

Nell had not intended to try to enter, but she did whisper, "May I get Tippy?"

Wallis shook her head. "He's curled up in Miss Allegra's lap. If I try to move him, it will disturb her."

There was nothing for Nell to do but to accept the situation. She nodded and said, "I'll check back later."

Nell walked away. She knew the effects of laudanum were long-lasting, and while she didn't know how large a dose Miss Benedict had given Allegra, Nell guessed Allegra would probably sleep most of the afternoon.

Nell was walking back to her room when Miss Benedict stopped her in the hall.

"I hope you now realize I was right about your choice of reading for Allegra. You don't seem to understand that Allegra is a sheltered, innocent, young woman, unaware of the world of highly charged emotion and sensationalized writing. I feel it is my duty to apprise Dr. Herbert of the kind of companionship you are giving his patient. I don't think he would be at all pleased."

Miss Benedict brushed past, leaving Nell feeling discouraged and depressed. Were all her efforts in vain? Was she a total failure? Had coming here been a terrible mistake?

Then, with a surge of indignation, Nell's resolve returned. Miss Benedict was taking advantage of Allegra's breakdown as a means of vindicating herself. Over the weeks Nell had been at Hope's End, she had noticed how the woman seemed to take pleasure in being spiteful. Nell had seen her reduce Wallis to tears, Jewel to helpless rage, Nanny to bewildered confusion. Nell realized she would do anything to undermine Nell's position.

The old adage "know thine enemy" came into Nell's mind. Miss Benedict was indeed a formidable enemy. Nell straightened her shoulders and told herself resolutely, *Well, she has met her match in me.*

*N*ell knew she would have to proceed with caution after Allegra's unexpected emotional reaction to the previous day's reading. The next afternoon she took the cribbage game Hamilton Lewis had helped her select.

"I thought this might be something you'd enjoy as a change of pace, Allegra," Nell said, showing her the cribbage board, the deck of cards. There was definitely a spark of interest in Allegra's eyes as Nell laid everything out. Nell took out the instruction book and began to read the rules to her. As usual, Miss Benedict, Wallis, and Nanny, all busy with handiwork, were there listening to every word.

Allegra caught on quickly and soon the game captured her attention. She eagerly waited for her turn to play her hand and move the pegs on the cribbage board. Nell was elated.

When it was time for Allegra's nap, Nell gathered up the board and the deck of cards and left the room. To her surprise, Wallis followed her out into the hall where she turned on her furiously.

"I am deeply shocked, Miss Winston, that you would introduce Miss Allegra to such a game. It may not be my place to say so, but it's wicked. Cards are the devil's own tools, and I am very much offended by what you've done."

Stunned, all Nell could do was protest, "It's only a game, Wallis. Allegra was having a good time. What harm can that be?"

"What harm? You'll see just what harm," she said smugly, then, glaring, she went back into Allegra's room, shutting the door with a firm click. It might as well have been the grating sound of a bolt and chain.

Another mistake? Another enemy? Nothing she did seemed to be right.

Longing to escape from the oppressive atmosphere that seemed to be closing around her, Nell rushed downstairs and out into the garden. It was a glorious early autumn day—bright sun, blue cloudless skies, air with just a taste of crispness. Deep in thought, Nell walked briskly down the path to the lake. What else could she do to overcome the resistance that surrounded Allegra? What more could she do to help her? Reaching the dock, she walked to the end and looked out over the lake. The water shimmered in the sunshine, glistening and sparkling. Nell breathed deeply, feeling invigorated. Wouldn't getting out into this beautiful weather do the same for Allegra? Shut up all the time in that overheated room with never a breath of fresh air could not be good for her.

As her conviction grew, Nell became determined that if no one else would do it, she would have to insist upon it herself. It shouldn't be that difficult. They could bundle Allegra up warmly, and Lawrence could carry her downstairs. The wheelchair was sturdy enough to be pushed easily along the garden paths. It would do Allegra a world of good, Nell was sure.

The next day, when she went for Tippy, with inner reservations she did not allow to creep into her voice, Nell spoke directly to Allegra. "It is a beautiful, sunny day. I want you to come with us today." Nell ignored the shock on the faces of the hovering Wallis and Miss Benedict. Nanny Maybank was also present, and, out of the corner of her eye, Nell thought she saw her nod her gray head in approval.

Allegra shrank back into the cushions. Her face had a startled expression, yet she did not refuse. Nell kept talking in a cheerful, firm manner. "It is really warm today. I'll ring for Lawrence to take down your chair, then carry you downstairs." To Wallis, she directed, "Get Miss Allegra's cape and a scarf for her head."

Wallis looked at Allegra, then back at Nell.

"I'm not at all sure you should, darling." Miss Benedict was at Allegra's side, bending over her solicitously, speaking in worried tones.

It was then Allegra cast the deciding vote. She waved Clarise away dismissingly and gave Nell a confirming nod.

Nell walked over to the fireplace and pulled the tapestry bell cord to summon Lawrence, whom she had already alerted; he came immediately. An obviously disapproving Wallis brought Allegra a cape, a shawl, and a knitted scarf, draping it around her all the while glaring at Nell. In silent fury, Miss Benedict, hands clasped tightly, watched the preparations with angry eyes. Nell knew she was likely insuring their wrath by what they considered her high-handedness. But it was for Allegra's sake. Someone had to do it. The phrase in her mind amended that to "Someone has to save Allegra." It should be a knight in shining armor on a white steed fighting the dragons to rescue the captive princess; but since there was no such person in sight, it was up to Nell.

The weather had kept its promise. It was a day for poets to wax lyrical. There was a winy scent in the air that made Nell light-headed. She had succeeded. She had managed to get Allegra out of that gloomy cave of a room, out into the bright fall sunshine. *Please, Lord, make her eager for more excursions . . . each one farther, longer,* Nell prayed.

Allegra was lightweight, and Nell pushed the wheelchair

easily along the garden paths. With the loop of his leash around Nell's wrist, Tippy walked alongside his mistress's wheelchair contentedly. It was such a happy experience, Nell began to feel justified in her bold step. But her complacency was short-lived. Beginning to feel confident, Nell decided it would be a good idea to wheel Allegra down to the stables. Perhaps if she saw Princess, the desire would return not only to walk but also to ride her beautiful horse.

Following her intuition, Nell turned the wheelchair around and headed down the path that led to the stables. But this time her inner direction proved wrong. All at once she was aware that Allegra was moving agitatedly: She waved her hands protestingly and shook her head vigorously from side to side. Nell stopped immediately, pulled the handbrake of the wheelchair, and ran around in front of Allegra. The young woman's face was distorted, her eyes wide with distress and filled with tears. She kept shaking her head as her mouth opened and shut with a soundless "no" over and over. Her shoulders began to shake as sobs wracked her whole fragile body. Then she put her head in her hands, crying as if her heart would break.

Panic-stricken and at a loss to know what had brought on this terrible emotion, Nell tried to comfort Allegra. She leaned over her, stroking her back as the sobs continued.

"Oh, what is it, Allegra? What's wrong?"

Allegra raised her tear-streaked face and pointed to the house in jerky thrusts.

"All right, yes, yes, we'll go back inside." Nell turned the wheelchair around and pushed it in the direction of the house. What had caused this storm when everything was going so smoothly? she asked herself frantically, knowing she would be asked the same question when she brought Allegra back in this condition. What might have triggered this outburst? When Allegra realized they were on the way to the stables, she had had a violent reaction. Perhaps it would be too painful to see the beloved horse she could no longer ride?

Then a daunting suspicion followed. Or was it that Allegra did not want to see Hugh Douglass?

As this possibility struck Nell, a chill went through her. Was there some romantic connection between Allegra and the stable master? An unrequited love on her part since Nell suspected where Hugh Douglass's real interest lay. Nell recalled Hugh Douglass's unabashed admiration of Felicity Selkirk's mare. How the affection for Sheherazade somehow included her mistress. Were the Selkirk cousins rivals for the same man? Nell was grieved that she had inadvertently caused Allegra more anguish.

Miss Benedict and Wallis, both stony-faced, were downstairs waiting for their return. When they took one look at Allegra, they went into a frenzy. Allegra was shivering. Nell knew it was from the emotional storm, but Wallis immediately declared, "She's taken a chill! I knew she shouldn't go out." She then lashed out at Nell.

Miss Benedict supervised Lawrence as he lifted Allegra from the wheelchair and followed them upstairs, but not before giving Nell a withering glance.

Nell was left alone with the empty wheelchair and Tippy, for once subdued and looking very forlorn. He sat on the floor beside her looking mournful as his mistress disappeared up the stairs.

Nell felt profoundly guilty. Even if she had acted out of the best intentions, the outing had been a disaster. She blamed herself for forging ahead. She had done something foolish, and now, not only she, but Allegra too would have to pay for it.

Nell did not know exactly what had awakened her, only that something had. She got out of bed and went to the door of her room. She peered out into the hall, which was dimly lit by a few gas lamps in wall sconces. The sound came again, muffled yet distinct. It reminded her of a small animal in distress or a pitiful cry like that of a child frightened by a bad dream. Nell stepped out a little farther, straining to see if she could tell from where it came.

Then, from some distance, she saw a figure moving silently on the carpeted corridor. It startled her, because it appeared to be not walking but gliding, like some disembodied wraith. Instinctively, she drew back into the frame of the door. As the apparition came closer, she saw with a shakily drawn breath that it was Wallis.

She was wearing a dark wine-colored wool wrapper, and her hair hung in a wispy plait over one shoulder. She was carrying a tray covered with a linen napkin.

Nell took a few steps forward and asked, "Wallis, is anything wrong? Can I help?"

Wallis halted, an annoyed frown puckering her forehead. She looked ahead toward Allegra's suite, then gave a quick look behind her. "Nothing I can't handle, miss. Miss Allegra rang for me and I'm taking her some hot milk and a sleeping draught. There's nothing at all for you to do, miss," she said nervously, then moved on.

"Haven't you done quite enough for one day?" a vicious voice demanded. Startled, Nell saw that Clarise Benedict was also a midnight wanderer.

Nell drew back, reprimanded by the accusation. Before she could think of something to say in her own defense, Miss Benedict hurried by. Defeated, Nell returned to her room.

She had made a mistake. She realized that. But had she ruined her chances to ever redeem herself in Allegra's opinion? That was all she cared about, all that was important. She only hoped she could persuade Allegra that she was trustworthy, that she wanted to be her friend.

Nell went back to bed and after a while to sleep. However, the encounters with Wallis and Miss Benedict must have been more upsetting to her than she realized, for she woke the next morning feeling headachy. She sat up in bed, her mouth dry, and with a general feeling of malaise. Jewel had not come with her breakfast tea as she usually did, so when

Nell was dressed, she ventured downstairs in search of a cup of reviving coffee.

As she rounded the landing, she saw Farnsworth had just opened the front door, and Dr. Herbert entered. At the same time, Mr. Selkirk emerged from his study and came forward to greet him. The two men conferred briefly in low tones. Then Dr. Herbert started up the stairs. Passing Nell, he gave her a cool nod and went on up the remaining flight of stairs. Mr. Selkirk saw Nell but did not speak and returned to his study, closing the door behind him.

Was this Dr. Herbert's regular day to see Allegra or had he been called? Had yesterday afternoon precipitated some sort of crisis that he had been summoned to attend her?

Nell's troubling thoughts were answered when she met Jewel, who was armed with a feather duster and broom and was heading toward the parlor.

"Oh, miss," Jewel greeted her with wide eyes. "Such a fuss; Wallis has been up most of the night with Miss Allegra. They sent Lawrence for the doctor first thing."

"What's the matter?" Nell asked, alarmed.

"They say Miss Allegra got a bad chill when you took her out yesterday," Jewel said in a hushed tone.

Nell felt thoroughly chastened. She realized she had hardened the feelings of Wallis and Miss Benedict against her and probably the Selkirks as well.

She found the coffee urn still on the sideboard in the dining room and poured herself a steaming cup. Her head was throbbing now.

"Miss Winston." Nell jumped at the sound of her name. She turned and saw Dr. Herbert standing in the doorway. "I'd like a word with you about my patient."

"Certainly." Nell set down her cup. The slight tremor in her hand caused it to rattle as she replaced it on its saucer. She got up and walked over to Dr. Herbert. Although Nell was tall, he seemed to tower over her intimidatingly.

"I understand your motives were of the best, Miss Winston. But inexperienced people often make errors of the worst kind." His tone of voice was mild, but there was a subtle disapproval in every word. "I commend your effort to persuade Allegra to vary her day appropriately. Getting out into the fresh air and sunshine was, in itself, commendable. However, one must always keep in mind the very delicate state of Allegra's health.

"Some people, self-ordained experts, I might add, have the idea of mind over matter. In my opinion, they are wrong. That kind of reckless theory can be very dangerous without any medical knowledge to substantiate their theories. And theories are all they are, Miss Winston. No scientific proof." He smiled at her almost indulgently. "I don't say we doctors have all the answers. Medicine continues to progress and learn. But I warn you not to plunge into unknown waters or you may do irreparable harm." He held up one hand as if to ward off any argument. "I know Gervase Montgomery has appointed himself as the guardian of Allegra's well-being. He has tried to insist on applying some newfangled notions to Allegra's condition. But he has interfered most incautiously and caused division in this family."

Again the doctor paused. "In my practice I have seen similar reactions to tragedy and loss as Allegra is manifesting. I also know that healing takes time. For someone as sensitive as Allegra, it may take longer. In her case—" here Dr. Herbert's voice had an edge Nell did not quite understand—"Allegra's grief is so intense because she was dependent on and devoted to her parents. Too devoted," Dr. Herbert added. "I hope you will keep in mind all that I've said."

With that, Dr. Herbert turned abruptly and returned to the foyer where Farnsworth was waiting with his overcoat and hat. Nell remained standing until he left and the door was shut after him.

His words resounded in her ears. Especially the last few. The way he had said "too devoted" had an edge to it, a bitter tone, a censorious tone. Can a child be too devoted? Isn't love for parents the first and strongest bond in anyone's life? How could it not be a tragic loss? Dr. Herbert's remarks seemed insensitive, even cruel.

Nell herself had lost a mother before she had any strong memory of her; yet something of that early love relationship had lingered in Nell's life—the faint melody of a lullabye, the haunting fragrance of lilies of the valley. Had that fragrance been from Grandmere's garden or had it been the perfume Mama wore? They were mingled, and, ephemeral as they were, she clung to them and never wanted to lose them.

Devotion too strong? Dr. Herbert was wrong. Nell could understand Allegra's loss. Maybe, no matter what the doctor or anyone else thought, *she* was the one who could help Allegra.

In spite of the disastrous outcome of our outing, and not knowing how Allegra would react, I went to take Tippy for his walk as usual. To my relief, as soon as he saw me, he sat up in Allegra's lap and gave a little bark. I held out my hand with the coiled leash in it, and Tippy jumped down and ran over to me. I looked at Allegra for permission, and she smiled and nodded. I was relieved. It seems Allegra, whatever the cause of her distress, does not blame me. Of course, Wallis and Miss Benedict maintain their icy wall of resentment, but I am just glad Allegra holds no grudge.

Something else happened today. Mrs. Russell has invited me to take tea with her tomorrow afternoon.

Nell knew that housekeepers in great houses held an unassailable position among the household staff. To have received an invitation to tea was a special honor. She realized this invitation bestowed a certain mark of acceptance, and she was grateful.

A little before four o'clock, Nell knocked at the door of Mrs. Russell's apartment with both curiosity and speculation of why she had been singled out so. She found out with Ada Russell, as it is often said, appearances are deceiving. Her first impression of the Selkirks' housekeeper had been of an austere woman, rather severe. However, during tea, Nell soon found her to be a woman of warmth and charm, easy to talk to and surprisingly eager to talk—about everything, including her employers. Perhaps she felt Nell's position, set apart from the others and more on a par with her own, made it safe to confide in Nell. Why else would she have been so forthcoming?

The housekeeper's rooms were pretty, very feminine, a mite fussy for Nell's taste, yet quite in keeping with what was popular: bouquets of dried flowers under glass domes, Dresden figurines on the mantelpiece, and a plethora of needlepoint—pillows, framed mottos, covers of books, and photograph albums. Needlepoint was obviously Mrs. Russell's handiwork of choice. A large wood tapestry frame stood prominently in a corner on which a needlepoint canvas of elaborate design was in progress, the needle and yarn at the place where her work had been halted.

Tea was laid out on a wheeled tea cart: a graceful porcelain teapot, cups and saucers decorated with pink roses, embroidered napkins bearing the monogram ABR, fluted dishes holding tiny triangular sandwiches of minced ham and cream cheese, dainty iced cakes, and a seed lemon loaf.

Mrs. Russell was elegantly dressed in her usual black, but today her jewelry was quite handsome. Jet-black earrings swung from her ears, and at her high, lace collar was pinned a large cameo, a black stone on which an ivory Grecian profile was imposed, surrounded by tiny pearls.

"So, Miss Winston, how are you getting along by now?" she asked in a friendly manner as she poured the tea.

"Quite well; at least I hope so," Nell answered, trying to be honest. "Allegra seems to accept me, and I hope we can be friends."

"Ah, such a sad case." Mrs. Russell sighed. "Of course, I never knew her before the accident. I only accompanied the Selkirks when they came to take over here. But I understand from what Miss Benedict tells me, there was never a livelier, more vivacious, fun-loving girl than Allegra." Mrs. Russell rolled her eyes heavenward. "Of course, she never met Miss Felicity. Now there's a lively one for you!"

From the tone Mrs. Russell used, Nell couldn't tell whether she admired or disapproved of the Selkirks' daughter. Mrs. Russell went on without Nell's having to comment.

"It's a strange situation here as you are finding out, my dear. My position is quite different than it was in the Selkirks' London home. I didn't know quite what to make of it when I first came. And poor cook, Mrs. Ellison, is unhappy and disgruntled. Not enough to do. No dinner parties, no entertaining. She's an excellent cook and a fine hand with pastry and feels her talent wasted. Since we came here, Mr. Selkirk lunches in the city and frequently doesn't come home for dinner."

She handed Nell the plate of petit-fours. Nell sampled one and remarked how delicious it was.

"I'll be sure to tell Mrs. Ellison. It's good to see someone with a healthy appetite. Miss Allegra picks at her food and sometimes sends her trays back to the kitchen untouched. But what do you expect? Allegra never gets out for any exercise or does anything to spark her desire to eat. I don't know how it's all going to turn out."

Mrs. Russell regarded Nell with an appraising look as if deciding whether to say more. After a small pause, she said, "I believe you will be good for Miss Allegra. Just what the doctor ordered, as they say." She halted, her mouth pursed for a few seconds, then, "I don't know about this doctor! Of course, it's not for me to say, but you'd think in all these months he'd have done something for her. Some special medicine, something to give her energy, wouldn't you think? Certainly not sleeping draughts or laudanum! She's sleeping her life away!" Mrs. Russell shook her head.

Although surprised at such frankness, Nell was gratified to know she was not alone in thinking something was very wrong in this household, something under the surface, hidden.

After they finished their tea, Nell thanked Mrs. Russell for a delightful visit and returned to her room. The afternoon had provided her with more food for thought about the household and particularly about Allegra's situation. It had reinforced her own determination to do everything she could to bring about a positive change.

12

By the middle of October, the weather had turned too windy, too wet, for Nell to suggest taking Allegra outside again. However, their times together and the reading sessions continued, and Nell felt their relationship was developing into a warm, affectionate friendship.

When *David Copperfield* came to a happy and satisfactory conclusion, Nell decided to select another novel for them to read together. Perhaps another Dickens, no matter what Miss Benedict thought. Allegra was an intelligent young woman and would certainly enjoy another complex story, full of the turns and twists for which Dickens's books were famous.

November was ushered in by a week of storms. Wind blew away the last leaves clinging to the trees, and rain slashed fiercely against the windows. Tippy would only permit the briefest necessary trip out around the garden. Once back in the house, he would strain at the leash, and, as soon as it was unfastened, make a beeline up the stairs back to Allegra's room. There he would climb up beside her, burrow into her afghan, and be peering out with his bright eyes when Nell found him.

Inclement weather or not, Nell felt too confined and had to get out for a walk every day. One morning, with the object of finding a new book for Allegra, Nell set off for the village. Maybe this time something humorous like *Pickwick Papers*. Allegra had laughed at the parts in *David Copperfield* about Mr. Macawber. Dickens always injected at least one character who was wildly funny. Nell knew her choice would depend on what was available at Mr. Ives's store.

Actually the selection itself was easy enough. There were only a few titles on the shelf. She vacillated between *A Tale of Two Cities* and *Great Expectations*, finally choosing *Great Expectations*, thinking it less probable to cause Allegra much emotional distress.

Nell spent some additional time browsing. She had not wanted to antagonize Wallis by bringing in the cribbage board again, but she still felt Allegra needed to engage in a variety of activities. Perhaps a jigsaw puzzle? Nell spent some time looking at the various ones in stock. Finally, she chose one depicting a lovely pastoral scene: sheep grazing in lush meadows, a sun-warmed stone cottage nestled in a flowered dell.

Nell had taken longer making her purchases than she had intended, and when she left the stationer's, she discovered the day had turned gray and overcast. As she started along the road back to the Selkirks', a sense of depression began to creep over her. The clouded sky reminded her to what she was returning—Allegra's room with its heavy draperies drawn against the outside world, shutting out the light; the gloomy hallways; the unfriendly atmosphere.

Although she was in no hurry to get back, she found herself hurrying. She had left the village far behind, and this was a lonely stretch of country road. At this time of day, there was no traffic; not a delivery cart, drover's wagon, or carriage was in sight. On either side loomed deep woods. She turned up the collar of her coat and quickened her pace.

A prickling on the back of her neck prompted a disturbing feeling that she was being followed. Every nerve was suddenly alerted. She looked over her shoulder but saw nothing. Still, her heart began to beat uneasily.

She walked faster, taking longer steps, stumbling a little as she did. Just ahead, she could see the faint outline of the house beyond the gates. She started to run, her breath coming in painful gasps. In a few minutes she'd be safely inside the gates. Reaching them at last, she pushed through them and slammed them behind her. Clinging to the railings, she peered back at the road. Was that a figure halted a short distance down the road? Or had the whole thing been her frenzied imagination? She prided herself on being a down-to-earth sort of person, not given to fears and silly fancies. She must be careful not to let her imagination run away with her.

She drew a long, steadying breath and walked the rest of the way up the driveway toward the house. Suddenly, she stopped. Against the darkening sky, the house looked strangely sinister.

As Nell stepped into the front hall, she saw Dr. Herbert and Miss Benedict standing at the foot of the stairway in deep conversation. His head was bent toward her. Her one hand rested on his arm; with the other hand, she was gesturing, as if punctuating whatever she was telling him. When they heard the outer door open and shut, they looked in that direction, startled as though caught in some kind of conspiracy. When Miss Benedict saw Nell, her face twisted into a smug expression, masking the blatant dislike Nell had felt from her.

Feeling like an intruder, Nell murmured an apology and attempted to pass them and mount the steps when Dr. Herbert's voice halted her.

"One minute, Miss Winston, if you don't mind. Where are you going?"

Nell turned, irritated at his dictatorial tone. "I was going up to Allegra. It is time for us to have tea together," she replied, even though she did not feel required to report her every movement to him.

"I think not," he said firmly. "Allegra's heartbeat was rapid today. I was forced to give her laudanum, and now Allegra is sleeping soundly and should not be disturbed."

Nell was outraged. Being constantly told one is fragile and delicate, a person will begin to think so themselves. In the short time she had known Allegra, Nell had sensed a deep core of strength in her. Dormant, perhaps, yet there. Healing was taking place even if it was not yet visible. This, due in part to their reading and discussing Dickens's great human stories. But she felt helpless before Dr. Herbert's professional power and Miss Benedict's self-righteous support of him.

"Very well," was all Nell managed to say before continuing up the stairs. In the hall, she met Wallis, who was pulling Tippy doggedly along.

"Do you want me to take him out, Wallis?"

Wallis hesitated; then, with evident relief, she nodded. "If you will, miss. I'd be grateful."

"Wait a minute until I put my things away, and I'll give him a quick run in the garden," Nell said and hurried to her bedroom. There she dumped her packages, shed her coat and hat. She would go down the back stairs to avoid the doctor and Clarise again. Go through the room that led out to the garden.

Out in the hall again, she took the leash from Wallis and hurried downstairs. She grabbed the ulster from its hook by the door and went outside. Tippy scurried ahead, then stopped to investigate something under a nearby shrub. Nell halted.

Finally Tippy came out, and they continued walking down the path toward the lake. Suddenly she heard a thrashing sound, and out of the shaggy bushes emerged the figure of a man. Nell stifled a scream and wheeled around, pulling the yipping Yorkie with her as she started to run. But the man caught her sleeve and held it, saying in a desperate voice, "Wait, please, Miss Winston. I mean you no harm. I must speak to you."

Her heart pounding, Nell gasped, "How do you know my name? Who are you?"

Facing her was a slim young man, well dressed and with as innocent an expression as one could imagine. His eyes were wide and pleading.

"Please, just listen. I overheard you in the post office. Perhaps I should have spoken to you then, but it was too crowded. My name is Carrick Rowe. I'm a friend of Allegra's. Well, before the accident—we were—" He paused, his voice cracking a little as he went on. "I love Allegra. And she loves me. At least, she did. Oh, Miss Winston, I don't know. I'm so miserable. They won't allow me to see her and—you're my only hope." His arms fell to his side limp, his whole figure one of dejection.

Something about Carrick Rowe was so sincere, so transparent, Nell had to believe him. When she caught her breath, she gasped, "You scared me half to death. Jumping out at me like that."

"I'm sorry. I tried to speak to you earlier. You were walking back to the house, and I had followed you from the village. I almost caught up with you when I saw the other person, and I knew you couldn't talk to me if it was one of the Selkirks." He halted. "But now I've been waiting so long. I'm so anxious to hear how Allegra is, to know . . ." he paused again. "Please, Miss Winston, I beg of you. I'm desperate for some information. They won't let me in the house. I've gone time after time only to be turned away. They won't take the flowers I bring; my notes are returned."

The anguish in his voice touched Nell's soft heart. Everything he said rang true. What he was describing sounded like the wall the residents at Hope's End had erected around Allegra. But why for this nice young man? Surely it would have been helpful to Allegra to have the person she loved, who loved her so much, visit her. Nell's indignation overcame her natural reluctance to accept the word of a stranger. "But what can I do?" she asked. "I cannot go against Allegra's uncle."

He drew an envelope from under his coat and held it out to her. "Could you please see that Allegra gets this?"

She hesitated. To become the go-between in a romantic situation, one that was forbidden for unknown reasons, was a dangerous step for her to take.

"Please, Miss Winston, you're my only hope. I love Allegra, and I know she still loves me. I'm afraid she thinks I've deserted her."

Nell remembered Allegra's plaintive remark about not hearing from her uncle Gervase. Could someone be intercepting her mail, witholding it?

"If you only knew the truth, Miss Winston, you'd help us."

The truth? What was the truth? Nell asked herself. At least she could hear Carrick's version.

"We better walk along farther, so as not to be seen from the house," she said cautiously, and together they moved down the path that led to the lake.

"Allegra and I," Carrick began, "were childhood sweethearts, you might say. We always knew we'd be together when we grew up, that we would marry and live happily ever after." At this his voice took on a sadness. "Allegra's parents were wonderful about it. Treated me as the son I was to become. I spent many happy times with all of them, already considered part of the family. Then the accident happened. Mr. and Mrs. Selkirk both killed, and Allegra . . ." His voice broke, and it took some effort for him to go on.

"For weeks Allegra lay mostly unconscious, paralyzed. She wasn't even able to attend their funeral. I watched the doctors come and go, the long faces. Then the Selkirks arrived. Desmond Selkirk, Allegra's father's brother, came first. Later, the wife and daughter, a caravan of carriages, wagon loads of their belongings, moved in. Then everything changed. That's when I was no longer allowed admission. I was sent away like some kind of tramp begging for food."

He stopped suddenly and turned to Nell, clenching his hands into fists. "I used to hide in the grounds; I knew a way to get in past the gates. After all, I'd played there as a boy, knew all the secret paths. Allegra and I had many hiding places, a tree house even, a great place for spying." He paused. "That's how I knew about you. I began to see you take out her little dog. Then I knew you must have become a friend or else Allegra would never have let Tippy go with you. I realized if I could only convince you to help me, you would be the key to Allegra. Oh, Miss Winston, I have to know. How is she? Is she getting better? Will she ever walk again?"

Nell looked into that longing face, those eyes yearning for a scrap of information about his beloved. How heartless the Selkirks had been to keep him from seeing Allegra. Instead of keeping them apart, bringing them together might have been the very thing to make Allegra want to walk again, be well, be assured that there was still the possibility of happiness for her.

"I don't think there's been much change. She still lies on her lounge most of the time. From there they carry her into bed. The doctor comes, but—I'm sorry, I really can't give you much information."

"I don't trust her uncle Desmond," Carrick said fiercely. "He's not at all like his brother. Allegra's father was a generous, genial, kind man. Of course, Allegra adored him, and he was my hero. My own father died when I was just a little boy, and Mr. Selkirk filled that role for me."

"Why don't you trust Desmond?" Nell pursued the subject, finding some support for her own suspicions of him.

"My stepfather has had some dealings with him over property lines. Found him to be arrogant, out to win, lacking certain traits one expects to find in a gentleman. Especially a country gentleman. He has business interests in the city that preoccupy him. No one seems to know why he decided to come down here and move into his brother's house. He doesn't love Hope's End really. Not like Allegra's father did."

Carrick hesitated, then, sounding agitated, went on. "I'm worried sick about Allegra being with them. I don't think they really care about her. Oh, they care about the house, the grounds; it's one of the finest estates in the county. And it belongs to Allegra, not Desmond, although he acts like he's the owner. If she knew I wanted to see her. . . . I wonder if she asks anybody about me. Or if she thinks I've deserted her."

"How can I help?" Nell asked impulsively. She was genuinely moved by the young man's obvious distress.

"Tell her you've seen me, what I'm trying to do; tell her I love her. Maybe if she knew, she'd make them let me see her. At any rate, see that she gets my letter."

He held it out again, and she took it. As if sensing her reluctance, Carrick said, "All I'm asking you to do is try."

"That's all I can do. We're never completely alone. Her maid, Wallis, is always in attendance, and then Miss Benedict—"

Carrick made a distasteful face. "The dragon. That's what we used to call her. She was always hovering, stalking us; wherever we went, there she was like a shadow, ready to pounce."

Nell had to smile; the dragon sounded like an apropos name for Miss Benedict. A picture formed of the mythical dragon keeping the fairy-tale princess prisoner. Suddenly aware of how long they had talked, Nell said, "I must be getting back. It's getting late."

A wistful look crossed Carrick's face. "Could we arrange to meet again so that you could tell me about Allegra? Maybe she'll answer my letter and let you bring it to me. I don't trust anyone there to mail it for her."

Thinking of the possible repercussions of meeting with someone to whom the Selkirks had forbidden access, Nell hesitated.

"It probably would be best not to meet in public."

"Then what about the dock at the lake at Hope's End?"

Carrick suggested. "Our house is just across the lake; Allegra and I used to meet there. I came across in my boat. It's easy, and we wouldn't be seen from the house."

"All right, but how will I know when you will be there?" Nell felt nervous. This was turning into a complicated plan.

"I'll get word to you. Surely, your mail isn't tampered with?"

"No, but—"

Carrick took both her hands in his, saying, "How can I thank you enough, my dear Miss Winston. You'll never know how much this means to me."

"I'll do what I can, Mr. Rowe, but I can't promise anything."

"I know, but at least I know you're on our side. Allegra's and mine. And you will tell her how much I care, that I love her and want us to be together again . . . and forever."

His passionate words rang in Nell's ears, resonated in her heart. Surely such a love as his would be restorative to Allegra.

"Again, I'll do what I can."

"That's all I ask. Thank you."

Clouds were gathering overhead, shadows were lengthening. Nell knew she would have to hurry inside. The heavy mist was thickening; gray strands lifted like floating ghosts from the lake.

Back in the house, Nell hurried upstairs to her room. The enormity of what she had done, what she had promised Carrick Rowe suddenly hit her. To become the messenger between him and Allegra was certainly not included in her job. Who had been the instigator of the refusal of visitation privileges to Mr. Rowe? And why? It was taking a great risk to believe this unknown young man. But some instinct made Nell believe his conviction that there was a conspiracy against him for some reason. What was at stake here? Allegra's happiness and well-being, Nell concluded.

There was something so genuine about Carrick Rowe. She felt instinctively he was a man of honorable character. His life and future had been almost as drastically altered by the accident as had Allegra's.

In these past weeks, Nell had become very fond of Allegra. There was something so poignant about her. Her patience, her acceptance of her condition underneath which must beat an aching heart had evoked a responding sympathy and admiration in Nell. How Allegra must long for the carefree, active, happy life she had lost, the one that now seemed out of her reach.

Yes, it would be worth it to help Allegra regain it. Whatever the cost, Nell decided she would go with her instinct in this matter and do what Carrick Rowe requested.

How was she to tell Allegra about her meeting with Carrick and slip her his letter? They were rarely by themselves long enough to impart such an important message. Somehow she must find a way.

Nell was still turning the matter over in her mind when the dinner gong sounded. When she entered the dining room, she saw to her dismay that Dr. Herbert was seated at his place of honor by Mr. Selkirk.

Nell had never gotten over her first impression of the doctor. It had neither changed nor improved by further contact. She couldn't explain why; it was just a distinctive prickling sensation she had in his presence, a feeling that there was some kind of darkness about him. His attitude toward her, when they encountered one another, was one of tolerant condescension. Nell had no other alternative than to try to avoid him whenever possible. But, like this evening, when he was here as the Selkirks' guest, this was impossible.

During dinner, the talk turned to the arrival of the Selkirks' daughter, Felicity, for the coming Christmas holidays and of a gala party they planned to give for her. Nell thought, *What a shame this party is not for Allegra, announcing her engagement to Carrick Rowe.* It was only a passing thought, and most of the discussion went in one ear and out the other. Nell was preoccupied as to how she could give Allegra Carrick's letter. Maybe she could wait until Wallis had gone downstairs to prepare Allegra's nightly milk, then slip into her room. That was probably the best way.

After dinner, Nell went to her bedroom. Filled with nervous excitement about all that had happened that day, she sat down at her desk, took out her journal, and wrote.

I honestly believe Carrick and Allegra should be allowed to see each other. It is cruel and unnecessary to keep them apart when they were so deeply involved before the accident. Someone is playing master puppeteer, jerking the strings and making people behave the way they would marionettes with no mind or will of their own.

Who is doing it? is the question. Allegra's uncle Desmond? For what purpose? Mrs. Selkirk? No. She is far too weak and spineless to stand up for the young woman's happiness. Or is it just that she is afraid of her husband?

Everyone around Allegra has some motive to keep her isolated, but what is it? Who possibly benefits from this state of affairs?

A knock on the door startled Nell. She put down her pen and called, "Yes, come in."

It was Jewel. "Not disturbing you, am I, miss?"

"No, not at all."

"Come to turn down your bed and bring you a carafe of water," Jewel said matter-of-factly. She set down the carafe and went briskly about, folding back the coverlet, smoothing the blanket.

Jewel usually had a lot to say, and tonight was no exception. Nell could see the girl was upset by the way she moved around, slapping the pillows, all the while her face bearing a pugnacious look. Nell knew if she waited, Jewel would eventually say what was bothering her. It soon came in a torrent.

"All this talk about Miss Felicity's coming brightening up the house, that's what the mistress calls it, don't ring true for us servants. What it means is a whole lot more work for everybody. Mrs. Ellison will have to fix special meals, snacks, orders for tea. I'll be carryin' up trays and jugs of hot water at all hours. Miss Felicity has her own time clock, she does . . . bathes whenever it suits her. And her room, like a cyclone it is, clothes thrown all over. One wearing and she's done with it. Ironing to be done over 'cause she tries on a dozen things, drops whatever she has on so's it gets wrinkled, and then decides that's the one she wants. Oh, I'll tell you, miss, it's going to be a jolly old holiday for the staff."

Although she sympathized, Nell said nothing. She had seen some of the guests at the inn behave the same way and heard the complaints of the chambermaids about them. They were always the same guests who left no tips for the extra service they demanded.

"Too bad she's not like Miss Allegra." Jewel sighed heavily. "There's an angel for you. I'd walk over burning coals to serve her, and that's the truth."

She stood for a minute, hands on her hips, looking around the room, then said, "Anything else you need, miss? No? Well, good night then, and have a pleasant sleep."

After Jewel was gone, Nell thought about the difference between the way the Selkirks were anticipating their daughter's homecoming and the household staff's reaction. Jewel's description made Nell curious to meet Miss Felicity herself and make her own judgment.

Nell undressed and put on her nightgown and robe. She lowered the gas jet on her lamp so no telltale light would shine out in the hall when she opened her door a few inches;

she needed to see when Wallis went downstairs to fix Allegra's bedtime milk.

While Nell waited, she prayed she would find the right words and Allegra would react positively. Out of habit, she reached for her Bible. Almost instinctively she turned to the Scripture that again seemed significant. Mark 4:22. "For there is nothing hid, which shall not be manifested; neither was any thing kept secret, but that it should come abroad." She herself was now involved in something that must be kept secret.

It seemed a long time until she saw Allegra's maid go by. Nell hurried to the door, watched Wallis's tall figure start down the first flight of stairs, then waited until she was at the landing and made the turn to descend the last, long flight of steps down to the lower hall. As soon as she thought it was safe, Nell hurried out the door, down the corridor to Allegra's suite.

Allegra was already in bed in the room beyond the sitting room. The door was ajar, and Nell paused for a moment. Through the angle of the half-open door, she saw that the light shining through the pink glass globe of the lamp on the bedside table gave Allegra's face a rosy tint. For a minute Nell could imagine how radiant Allegra must have been when that was a real healthy glow. How sad that this young woman had been cut down at the peak of her youth and beauty. It made Nell more determined than ever to relay Carrick Rowe's messages to her.

Not wanting to startle Allegra, Nell tapped gently on the door. When Allegra looked up, Nell slipped in and over to the bed and perched on the side. She took both Allegra's hands in her own, leaned forward, and whispered, "Allegra, today in the garden, I met Carrick."

At this, Allegra's eyes widened and her mouth parted in surprise. Nell rushed on. Wallis could come back at any minute, cutting short this private time.

"He has been in an agony of suspense about you. He has

been haunting the house and grounds hoping to get word to you or about you. Did you know your uncle and aunt have kept him from seeing you?"

Allegra frowned slightly but then withdrew one of her hands from Nell's grasp and pointed her finger at herself. Nell understood then that it was Allegra's choice not to see Carrick.

"But why, Allegra? He adores you. He wants to help you get well so that you can be together as you planned. You need someone who loves and cares and wants to support you; don't you see that?"

Tears welled up in Allegra's eyes, making them more luminous. She shook her head and bit her lower lip. Then she reached for the pad and pencil always near at hand. She grabbed it and quickly wrote something, then handed it to Nell to read.

"I can't bear for him to see me like this. How could he want me now, a paralyzed mute?"

Tears streamed down the pale face. Deeply moved by Allegra's emotion, Nell longed to put her arms around her, comfort her. Just then they heard footsteps, and a minute later, Wallis, tray in hand, stood in the bedroom door. Her expression was a mixture of resentment and disapproval.

"Miss Winston, what is the meaning of this? I had Miss Allegra all settled for sleep. Why have you come in at this hour? It looks as though something you've said or done has upset her."

Allegra wiped her eyes with the back of her hands, touchingly childlike, and shook her head vigorously as if to deny Wallis's accusations. She reached for Nell's hand, squeezed it, then scribbled "Thank you" on the bottom of the sheet of paper on which she had written. When Nell read it, she nodded, and Allegra tore off the page and crumpled it up.

Wallis stood like a statue, her face carved in reproof. Impulsively, Nell leaned down and kissed Allegra's cheek. As she did, she quickly slipped the letter from under her robe and slid it under Allegra's covers. "Good night. Sweet dreams." Then she got up, went past Wallis without explaining her visit, and left the room.

As Nell stepped into the corridor, which was only dimly lit by the wavering light from the widely spaced gas lamps along the wall, she paused for a minute. She heard a door closing down the hall.

Nell shivered. Had someone been standing outside Allegra's room listening while she had told her about the clandestine meeting with Carrick Rowe?

13

*T*he next day, when Nell came for their usual reading session, Allegra gave no signal, not even the slightest look or gesture, to acknowledge Nell's visit the night before. Nell was puzzled but on further thought came to the conclusion that Allegra was practiced at concealing her emotions. Maybe she had closed off that part of herself so completely. Had she shut off all remembrance of what she and Carrick had shared just as she had shut herself away from the life she had lived before the accident? Nell wondered, had she been wrong to take Allegra his heartfelt plea? Instead of giving her hope, had it saddened her heart? Nell hoped she had not done her harm and tried to be optimistic that some good would come of the reckless promise she had made to Carrick.

Two days later, when the first post came in the morning, Farnsworth laid it out in his usual manner on the hall table in separate piles for each of the addressees. Nell was dismayed when she came down for breakfast to find Miss Benedict surveying the envelopes. She looked up at Nell's approach, and with what could only be described as a smirk, remarked, "You seem to be the popular one this morning, Miss Winston. A veritable windfall of mail for you."

Ignoring the sarcasm, Nell walked over to the table and picked up three letters addressed to her—one from Aunt Hester, one from Grandmere, and the third in a script unidentifiable to her. She guessed it might be from Carrick and wondered, if by any chance, Clarise Benedict recognized the handwriting.

"I could not help but notice the foreign stamp," Miss Benedict said, affecting a casual interest while her eyes narrowed curiously.

Astonished that the woman would so readily admit having snooped at someone else's letters, Nell gathered up her mail and, without giving any further explanation, took that envelope and waved it a little. "My grandmother. France."

"Ah, how—quaint," Miss Benedict said lamely. "I have a friend who is quite a stamp collector. Perhaps, if you have no need for the stamp yourself, you might give it to me to send to her?"

Nell merely looked back at her with as blank an expression as she could manage. The gall! She almost retorted, "Perhaps you'd like to read the letter as well?" Instead, she merely shrugged and went back upstairs where she could read her letters in private.

The letter in question *was* from Carrick; his note to her was brief.

> I will never be able to thank you enough for what you are doing. Bring the reply—and I pray to God Allegra will reply— to me at the dock by the lake at the end of the property. I'll wait there Thursday afternoon at three o'clock.
> Yours,
> Carrick Rowe

Nell read the letters from her aunt and from her grandmother. Both brought back the warmth and goodness of these two households, which at different times she called home. Such a contrast to the one where she was now. She put the letters into the desk drawer and saw her personal journal. She brought it out and read over a few pages.

Allegra seems an intelligent young woman, fully conscious of her condition and yet obviously melancholy. The household here at Hope's End seems united in one goal: to keep Allegra secluded, protected from all outside influence.

Dr. Colin Herbert, Allegra's attending physician, seems competent enough, but I find him lacking in any humanity, compassion. I feel Allegra needs encouragement, inspiration. None of the people serving her seem to have qualities that would bring this about.

Nell sighed. She felt so helpless. She was failing in what Gervase had entrusted her to do. Maybe she should write another letter to him, tell him what she had observed. She sighed deeply. Would it be best for her to simply leave Hope's End? To give up what appeared to be a futile endeavor? Should she contact Gervase Montgomery and submit her resignation?

Nell dipped her pen into the inkwell and wrote furiously in her journal for a few minutes. She poured out her feelings. "Instead of helping Allegra, the persons supposedly devoted to her are hindering her recovery." Her pen flew over the pages as she recklessly wrote opinion after opinion.

Reading it over, she thought it would be wise to wait a day or two before sending a letter to Gervase. She closed her journal and returned it to the desk drawer.

Allegra had not yet given her a reply to Carrick's letter, which Nell had managed to give her earlier. Nell decided she would somehow have to ask her if she intended to do so. Of course, the problem was giving Allegra a chance to communicate her real feelings to Nell.

Perhaps later Allegra might indicate something. However, after dinner when Nell went upstairs to say good night, Allegra seemed agitated. To her dismay, Wallis was there. Nell had hoped she might have been downstairs in the pantry readying Allegra's bedtime snack tray. But there she was, moving busily about the room, doing unnecessary tidying.

At Nell's entrance, Tippy raised his head then settled back into the curve of Allegra's arm, the edge of the afghan flopped over one eye. Allegra motioned to Nell, and Nell went over to her. From underneath the afghan, Allegra drew an envelope, held it out to Nell.

Nell had just time to slip it into her bodice before the door opened and Clarise Benedict and Dr. Herbert entered the room.

The change in Allegra was startling. Nell noticed a tremor go all through her thin body as she drew back against the pillows.

Why had Clarise brought the doctor up this evening?

"Dr. Herbert wants to see you, Allegra, dear," Miss Benedict said. "He's been concerned that perhaps you are doing too much, being too stimulated." At those words she cast an "I told you so" glance at Nell.

"Just want to listen to your heart a little, my dear," Dr. Herbert said, coming over to Allegra and blocking Nell, who had to step away to allow him to pass.

Clarise hurried to place a chair beside Allegra so he could sit down. He drew his stethoscope from his medical bag, adjusted it to his ears, then leaned and placed it on Allegra's chest. For a few minutes everything in the room was still, listening, waiting. Finally, Dr. Herbert leaned back, removed the metal tubing from his ears. He gave Allegra a long, evaluating look, shook his head slightly, then got a small bottle from his satchel.

"I'm afraid my intuition was correct, my dear. Your heartbeat is very rapid tonight. Much more so than I like to hear. I'm going to give you a light sedative that will make you sleep soundly and give your poor little heart a chance to rest." He turned and stared at Nell. "I think it best there be no reading tonight or for that matter in the foreseeable future. Too exciting for a patient who needs a full night's sleep." He glanced at the book lying on the table near Allegra's chair. His long fingers touched the title. "*Great Expectations,* eh?" he murmured. "Well, perhaps, Miss Winston, it is *you* who have great expectations. You have been stretching Allegra's capacity, her endurance. You have no understanding of the damage her body has taken, how long it needs to rebuild its defenses."

Nell was indignant. There was so much implied in everything Dr. Herbert said, so much concealed in his professional voice, the calm, reasonable tone. Also there was no possible opposition. He was laying down the law. His instructions, Nell was sure, would be recorded by Miss Benedict, relayed to the Selkirks. Nell was to be chastised, then locked out, so the circle could then re-form around Allegra.

She looked at Allegra. Surely she would protest—write on her pad that he was wrong, that she enjoyed the reading, the cribbage games, her time with Nell. Nell knew Allegra couldn't explain her increased heart rate. But, of course, it was because of her excitement at her decision to let Nell take a reply to Carrick. That was the reason, but Nell could not reveal that.

Besides, Allegra did look wan. Her face was pale, her expression apathetic. She did seem as if she needed some medical help.

"I suggest you leave now, Miss Winston. I will administer the sleeping draught, and Miss Benedict can remain here with Allegra until she falls asleep."

Helpless to do anything but comply, Nell stepped over to Allegra's chair, took one of her hands, squeezed it, then leaned down and kissed her cheek, whispering, "Don't worry.

I'll take care of the note." Aloud she said, "Good night, Allegra, sweet dreams."

Miss Benedict did not meet her glance but stood expectantly poised beside the doctor while Dr. Herbert measured out a clear, gray liquid into a glass. Like the sorcerer's apprentice.

The thought sent involuntary chills down Nell's spine. Was Dr. Herbert some kind of Svengali with the former governess compelled to do his bidding? And how did this affect Allegra? The answer came unbidden. For good or evil? Maybe that was too severe a judgment, the analogy too bizarre, too medieval, too reminescent of malevolent masters, deadly potions, wicked plans.

Back in her own bedroom, Nell's resentment of the way she had been banished from Allegra's room turned to deep sympathy for Allegra. The victim. She must find some way to help her. But how?

Nell drew out Allegra's letter to Carrick she had hidden beneath her buttoned bodice. She held it for a minute or two. What did it contain? She hoped it said all the things she knew Allegra felt in her heart for Carrick. Maybe this would be the key to unlock the tower in which Allegra languished.

I have now become a go-between for the two star-crossed lovers, just like a character in a Shakespearian play. I have met Carrick twice on my walks with Tippy down by the lake and passed along letters from Allegra. Who knows where all this will end? And what my part in this melodrama will cost me?

The day Felicity Selkirk was to arrive for the holidays, the household was in a flurry. The servants were flying around in a frenzy of activity. Even Mrs. Selkirk was up early conferring with Mrs. Russell and the cook. It was easy for Nell to slip out of the house unnoticed and walk to the village. She had written a letter to Gervase and needed to send it.

Nell was deeply troubled about Allegra and the continued resistance of Miss Benedict and Wallis to prevent her visits or at least cut them short. It seemed they had become even more vigilant.

In the village, Nell stopped briefly at the post office before heading to the fabric store. She purchased some needles, embroidery thread, and examined some samples of velvet.

When she emerged, she continued down the street to window-shop. Some of the store windows already had displays of Christmas wares, and Nell lingered in front of them.

Suddenly she realized she had walked the entire length of the street and from there the train station was in view. She saw the Selkirks' carriage parked in front and remembered that Felicity was due to arrive that afternoon. Nell didn't know on which train or at what time. She was surprised to see Hugh Douglass pacing up and down the train platform. Why was *he* here? Only that morning, as Mr. Selkirk was leaving to catch his train into the city, Nell had heard him give orders to Milton, the coachman, to be sure to meet Miss Felicity's train that afternoon. So, why was Hugh Douglass here instead?

Even as she wondered, Nell caught a glimpse of a swirl of royal blue sweep around the side of the station house; then she saw a flash of a silver fox muff as a young woman flung herself into Hugh's arms. She watched in stunned amazement while the embrace lengthened.

So, her guess about Hugh Douglass being enamored with Felicity Selkirk had been right. And what she had wondered about was also answered: Felicity obviously returned the stable master's feelings. Nell, deep in thought, turned and started walking back up the street.

Reaching the top of the hill, she saw Milton, recognizable in his green, gilt-trimmed livery, emerge from The White Knight pub looking a little flushed. A trade must have been arranged; perhaps the passing of a few shillings to close the deal between driver and stable master?

Nell was in no hurry to return to Hope's End. Shut out from Allegra's room and not wanting to be caught up in the frantic activity elsewhere in the house, she decided to stop at the Buttercup Tearoom before the long walk back.

As she was about to enter, she saw a familiar figure heading her way. Hamilton Lewis. As he approached, he waved his hand. His expression of surprised pleasure made her heart trip. Coming up to her, he tipped his hat, smiling.

"Miss Winston, what brings you out on such an inclement day? Whatever it might be, it is my good fortune."

Nell cautioned herself not to be silly. Hamilton's courteous manner was natural to him. It meant nothing special, indicated no personal interest in her, but nonetheless it pleased her.

"Some errands," she replied. "And now a cup of tea."

He glanced up at the cloudy sky and remarked, "It looks as if we might have snow sometime soon. I would offer you a ride back to the Selkirks', except I am meeting my mother on the next train from London. She is coming down to the country for the holidays." He paused. "I would very much like for the two of you to meet."

Nell stilled the sudden racing of her pulse by reminding herself of the social distance that stretched between herself and Lady Anne Lewis. "Thank you, but I must get back to the house before Allegra wakes from her nap. We read together then have tea."

"She is no better then?"

"Not very much."

"I'm sorry to hear that." Hamilton frowned. His eyes were concerned. "I remember her so differently, a vivacious charming girl who could ride all day and dance half the night. It is really too bad."

For a moment, Nell wished she could unburden her worries about Allegra and the situation at Hope's End. But it would not be wise to do so. Not even to someone as sympathetic and kind as Hamilton seemed to be. She must not be tempted to confide in someone she hardly knew.

The sound of a train whistle in the distance echoed through the clear, cold air. Hamilton glanced toward the station.

"That could be Mama's train. That is, if she did not miss it." He smiled indulgently. "My mother tends to be casual about time schedules. But just in case, I better be there to greet her." Hamilton bowed slightly. "It was very nice to see you again, Miss Winston. Do give Allegra my kindest regards."

They said good-bye, and he set off in the direction of the station house. Nell walked up the street to the tearoom, a smile lingering on her face. How nice to be treated with such gallantry. Made her almost feel like a duchess.

She ordered a pot of tea and a scone. While she waited to be served, she once more became deeply thoughtful about the crisis at Hope's End. And it was a crisis. She felt she was standing in exact opposition to the powers that be— Desmond Selkirk and Dr. Herbert. It was only because of the fact that she had been hired by Allegra's guardian, Gervase Montgomery, that she had any support at all. Otherwise she was sure she would have been dismissed.

The waitress came, placed the warm currant scone in front of her, and poured her a cup of tea. She had just taken a few sips when someone spoke her name.

"Miss Winston." She looked up and saw it was Hamilton. This time he was accompanied by a tall woman swathed in sable furs. The family resemblance was unmistakable. This must be Lady Anne, Hamilton's mother. A web of tiny lines around her eyes and mouth were the only signs of age in a face that by any standard was still beautiful. Smiling as Hamilton introduced her, she held out one hand cordially to Nell.

"May we join you? I forgot my tea basket when I left London, and I am absolutely famished. Hamilton suggested we stop in here so I could sample the scones he says are superb, and I'm perishing for a cup of tea."

She made it all sound so happenstance that Nell almost believed her. However, she was sure Hamilton had taken note of her remark that she was going to have tea before heading back to Hope's End.

Hamilton held the chair out for his mother to sit down.

She shrugged off her fur scarf, and Nell saw the exquisitely woven cranberry traveling suit underneath. Lady Anne's dark hair was swept back under a velvet hat trimmed with ribbon and blue feathers. She wasted no time getting to the subject. "Hamilton tells me you are companion to Allegra Selkirk. What a pity what's happened up there. I've known her all her life, and I knew her parents too. A wonderful couple. It was a happy place then. They were so in love with each other and their little girl. To think of the tragedy of it all." Lady Anne sighed.

"I don't know whether Hamilton told you, but I grew up here. My family has been here forever. I played with the Selkirk brothers as well as the children in the village." She turned to Hamilton. "Order our tea and scones, darling." Then she went on talking. "I know all the rumors, all the stories, even though I spend half the year in London.

"I have known Colin Herbert from the time he was a boy, son of the village schoolmaster." She lowered her voice slightly. "Another tragedy, my dear. Colin was madly in love with Allegra's mother before she married. He was crushed when she chose to marry Matthew instead. Colin had become a doctor mainly to make something of himself so he could ask for her hand. Of course, the old colonel would never have allowed that. I never saw anyone as heartbroken as Colin Herbert on Matthew and Henrietta's wedding day."

Hamilton returned with a waitress carrying a tray on which was a fresh pot of tea and a basket of scones. The conversation turned to Allegra again, and Nell confided she had run out of ideas to amuse and interest her.

"Why don't you get a travel book for her?" Hamilton suggested. "One of some faraway place like Italy or Greece? Together you could plan a dream trip. Work out all the details of travel as if you were actually taking the journey. Plan everything—methods of transportation, side trips, tourist attractions, hotels, resorts . . . all that sort of thing."

"What a splendid idea, darling!" his mother exclaimed, clapping her hands. "Isn't he marvelous?" She beamed at Nell. "Hamilton is my imaginative, sensitive son. He gave me so many wonderful ideas when his father was laid up most of last winter. And they all worked."

Over the rim of her teacup, Nell sensed Hamilton's steady gaze. Suddenly it was hard to breathe. His mother's comments seemed to confirm her own reason for being so drawn to him, even on such slight acquaintance. There was a sensitivity, a thoughtfulness in him beyond the veneer of good looks, and good manners—the very qualities his mother appreciated and acknowledged.

Nell reminded herself that such thoughts could tempt her, and abruptly she said she must be going. As the trio left the tearoom, a few snowflakes were lazily drifting down from gray clouds.

"Snow!" exclaimed Lady Anne. "How I love it! Some of my happiest memories are of playing in it as a child."

Hamilton smiled at Nell as if in tender amusement at his mother's childish joy. Nell thought it was endearing, and Hamilton's obvious fondness for his mother made him seem even more charming.

"Can't we give you a lift back to the Selkirks'?" he asked.

"No, thank you," Nell protested. "Like you, Lady Anne, I find being outside in the snow quite delightful."

Hamilton laughed, and Lady Anne exclaimed, "Ah, a kindred spirit. But surely, at least to the gates? We pass right by there."

Feeling it would seem silly to refuse, Nell agreed and accompanied them into their carriage. Lady Anne kept up a lively conversation until they reached the gates. When the carriage stopped, Lady Anne said, "Do give Allegra my affectionate good wishes. I would love to come for a visit whenever she feels up to it."

Hamilton got out and assisted Nell down. He held her hand a little longer, saying, "It was very enjoyable seeing you again, Miss Winston. I'll see you next week at the Christmas party."

Nell did not think it proper to remind him she would hardly be included in the Selkirks' guest list. She just said, "Thank you, Mr. Lewis." He opened the gate for her, then rejoined his mother, and the carriage drove away.

For some reason Nell felt a lightness she had not felt in a long time, but she quickly reminded herself not to be misled. This brief encounter with Hamilton and his mother was nothing but an enjoyable happenstance. Nothing more. *Don't get any foolish ideas,* she told herself sternly.

Nell took the shortcut she'd discovered that led by the stables. There another segment of the story to which she had been an inadvertent witness unfolded. As she rounded the bend of the path leading up to the house, she saw Hugh Douglass and the young woman dressed in blue mount the outside steps to the stable master's quarters above the stables.

Nell averted her eyes and hurried past, hoping neither of them would turn and see her. Another secret, another undercurrent in this house that seemed to have its cache of them. When she came inside the house, she found Milton explaining to Farnsworth that Miss Felicity had not been on the train he met. Mrs. Selkirk came to the door of the morning room, evidently expecting to welcome her daughter, and overheard the discussion. Farnsworth repeated Milton's story, and Mrs. Selkirk, looking confused, said vaguely, "Oh, dear, perhaps I didn't get it right. Felicity told me what train she was taking, but I don't remember. I may have mixed it up. I don't know now where I put her letter." Mrs. Selkirk fluttered her hands in the direction of her cluttered desk behind her. "Well, no matter, there are only two more trains from London today. Milton, just go back to the station and meet the next one; if she's not on it, wait there." Mrs. Selkirk looked worried. "I do hope she gets here before Desmond." The frightened look she inevitably got at the thought of her husband's displeasure crumpled her pink face.

Nell went past them up the stairway, relieved that she had no part in this complicated alibi. A quotation learned in early childhood repeated itself in her mind: "What a tangled web we weave, when first we practice to deceive." Lies upon lies always demanded a terrible price.

At Allegra's tea time, Felicity still had not arrived. Nell was not concerned. Whatever the Selkirks' flighty daughter was up to was none of her business. She had enough on her mind. As they took tea, Nell told Allegra of her meeting with the Lewises and that Lady Anne had sent her kind regards. Allegra wrote on her pad, "She was a dear friend of my mother's." Nell started to tell her that Lady Anne had suggested she would love to come and visit but Allegra looked so pensive she decided to wait for another time. Just then Wallis arrived with Allegra's supper tray and Nell left.

15

That evening when Nell came down to dinner, she saw that Dr. Herbert and Miss Benedict were with the Selkirks in the drawing room. As she walked in to join them Mrs. Selkirk was explaining, "Milton waited for two trains, Desmond, then returned home. I instructed him to go back for the five-twenty. Felicity should certainly be on that."

So Felicity had not yet put in an appearance. *Is there no clock in the stable master's quarters?* Nell wondered. *Of course, lovers notoriously lose track of time.*

Desmond's face looked like a storm cloud, and he said gruffly, "Well, no matter. If she isn't here in fifteen minutes we'll go in to dinner."

He was noticeably annoyed. Mrs. Selkirk looked anxious, and Miss Benedict glanced nervously toward Dr. Herbert, who was sipping an aperitif and observing the scene with amused calm. An uncomfortable silence fell, which no one attempted to relieve. Then the hall clock struck the quarter hour, and Mr. Selkirk pulled out his ornate gold pocket watch, looked at it, clicked it shut, and announced, "We'll go in now."

Everyone was already seated at dinner when the front door opened and a gust of wind swept into the house causing the flames of the candles on the table to flicker and almost go out.

"What the devil—" Mr. Selkirk bellowed, pushing back his chair angrily just as a beautiful young woman rushed into the frame of the dining room doorway. Everyone turned to look at her.

"Papa! Mama!" she exclaimed. Whirling into the room, she stopped to plant a light kiss on her startled mother's cheek then skimmed around the table to where her father stood bristling. "Papa, dear!" she cooed; then on tiptoe she reached up and patted his cheek.

"What has kept you, my girl?" Mr. Selkirk demanded in a voice considerably softer than his first reaction to her late arrival.

"Oh, Papa, such a bother. A mix-up of trains in London, a change of schedules, then delays along the way, something to do with the track or—" she gave a little shrug. "Who knows? You ask and nobody seems to know why." She then glanced around the table bestowing a radiant smile. "What does it matter? I'm here; that's what's important."

"Sit down, darling," her mother urged, signaling to Farnsworth to bring Felicity her soup, the course on which the rest had already begun. With a swish of ruffled skirt, Felicity found the place that had been set for her and sat down. It was directly across from Nell who had a chance to take a good look at her.

In spite of the smooth excuse about late trains, mistaken schedules, Felicity had the definite look of someone just come from a rendezvous with a lover. If Nell had not seen them together, would she have guessed? Nell had seen enough honeymoon couples at Seaview Inn to recognize the starry eyes, the high color in the cheeks, the soft look of a rosy mouth that has recently been kissed.

As Felicity engaged her mother in an animated conversation, Nell took a second look, noting the perfection of features, the feathery eyebrows arched above the violet blue eyes, the flawless complexion, the glistening gold ringlets falling naturally behind delicate ears from which swung pearl drop earrings. Amazing, she thought, that behind that angel face was a duplicitous nature. Beauty and deceptiveness, always a dangerous combination.

The table conversation turned to plans for the gala Christmas party the Selkirks were giving. During most of this, Felicity seemed disinterested. Obviously she was thinking of something else. Or, more likely, someone else.

It was only when her mother asked her directly, "Don't you think so, Felicity, dear?" that she snapped back.

Looking from one parent to the other, she tried to get the gist of the discussion she had missed. Her mother prompted, "Your father wants to know if you have anyone you want to add to the guest list."

"Never mind who else," Mr. Selkirk said. "I want you to pay particular attention to Thomas Lewis."

Nell's ears pricked up at the name. Thomas, of course, was Hamilton Lewis's younger brother. It was Thomas who had asked specifically when Felicity was expected home. Felicity rolled her eyes dramatically. "Oh, Papa! Thomas is such a bore. He follows me around and hovers constantly. Do we have to include him?"

At this, Dr. Herbert gave a derisive little laugh and remarked, "Ah, Miss Felicity, how tiresome it must be for you to have so many young men adoring you."

Felicity tossed her head and gave him a look that was half-indignant. "Can I help it if my friendliness is mistaken for flirtaciousness? Thomas is hopelessly young and inexperienced."

"So you prefer older men, eh?" Dr. Herbert chuckled, baiting her.

Nell saw Miss Benedict stiffen and throw an acid look at Felicity. She seemed to resent any attention the doctor paid to anyone—especially any woman younger than herself.

What would she think if she knew Felicity's interest lay elsewhere? Felicity probably had none whatsoever in Colin Herbert, thought him much too old. Felicity simply had a natural inclination to flirt with any male.

At this exchange, Desmond scowled and said to his daughter, "Well, the Lewises have an older son, if it comes to that. Either would make a most eligible suitor."

To her own amazement, Nell felt immediate chagrin. She couldn't imagine Hamilton Lewis being interested in someone as shallow as Felicity.

"Enough of this nonsense," Desmond continued. "Just mark my words, young lady; your butterfly days are over, and it is about time you thought seriously about your future. Just keep in mind, I want you to give young Lewis special courtesy. His father is an important business associate of mine."

"Desmond." A warning note in his wife's voice from the other end of the table made his frown deeper. "No more need be said right now."

His face reddened, but he said nothing more.

Felicity, however, was pouting. She got to her feet and, flinging her napkin down, said in an offended tone of voice, "Of course, Papa, whatever you say. Now may I be excused? I am tres fatigued; that's French, Papa. It means I am very weary from my trip."

Desmond caught the insolence in her reply, and his color deepened. With difficulty, he curbed his temper.

Felicity started to leave. As she passed her mother, Millicent reached out and caught her arm. "Be sure to stop by Allegra's room and say hello to your cousin, dear."

With a pained expression and an exaggerated sigh, Felicity nodded, then flounced out of the room.

Upon her departure, a heavy silence fell. The only sound was the clink of silverware against china as everyone tried to resume their meal. The small contretemps between father and daughter probably was only a minor crack on the surface that concealed even stronger conflicts.

Wallis had come down with a heavy cold, and so it fell to Nell to prepare Allegra's evening snack of milk and biscuits. Although sorry that Wallis was sick, Nell thought that this might give her the opportunity to be alone with Allegra.

When she went into the pantry to fix the tray, she could clearly overhear the voices from the adjoining kitchen, of Milton complaining to the cook, "She weren't on the five twenty from London. I dinna see exactly where from but she come runnin' onto the platform from somewheres else."

"She's alyus been a sly one, she has," Mrs. Ellison replied. "Even when she was a li'l un she'd slip around behind their backs. And they none the wiser. More's the pity."

Nell turned to look through the door that led into the warm, bright kitchen. To her surprise, she saw Hugh Douglass sitting at the long scrubbed oak table. The cook placed a bowl of stew and dumplings in front of him and went on talking. "I alyus sez she'd come to grief with her headstrong ways. It's the missus I feel sorry for. She fair dotes on the lass. Her one and only."

Fascinated, Nell stood there. Everything the cook, who had known Felicity all her life, was saying confirmed what Nell instinctively had felt even with her brief encounter.

She saw Hugh's neck and face slowly turn red. He picked up his spoon and began eating as if indifferent to the discussion.

So far, it seemed the lovers had been able to keep their romance a secret. Even from the household staff. That in itself was quite a trick. Nell knew the folks "downstairs" were usually pretty well aware of whatever the people "upstairs" were doing. How long Felicity and Hugh would be able to keep their relationship a secret was the question.

16

O n her way back up to Allegra's room with the tray, Nell mulled over the conversation she had over-heard. When she reached the top of the stairs, she saw the door to Mrs. Selkirk's room was ajar and heard a loud, angry voice. "I won't! I won't be sold off like one of Papa's stocks! I don't care. You can't make me."

Nell froze. Eavesdropping was reprehensible; yet here, she seemed always trapped in the role she despised. If she moved, a floorboard might creak; if she tried to go past, she might be seen and suspected of listening. Anything could give her away.

Nell looked around for a way to escape. But the door had somehow opened farther so that she could clearly see into the room. She saw Desmond's massive figure pacing back and forth. If she moved an inch either way she might be caught. She tiptoed over to a windowed alcove and pressed herself against the heavy draperies. There was nothing else she could think of to do.

Mr. Selkirk's harsh voice came. "You'll do exactly what you're told, young lady. You are not of age and you have no resources of your own. So don't play high and mighty with me."

"Mama!" Felicity's trembling voice appealed. "Surely you don't agree with Papa?"

"Your mother has nothing to say in this matter," said Mr. Selkirk. "I make the decisions in this family."

"Mama!" Felicity pleaded again.

"Dear child, we have no choice," Mrs. Selkirk replied in her usual ineffective manner.

"Can't Papa sell something? What about some land? There are acres and acres of no use to anyone—"

"All of which belong to your cousin Allegra," came Mr. Selkirk's edgy retort. "My brother's will left everything to his daughter in trust of a guardian, her uncle Gervase Montgomery, until she is twenty-one."

The way he said Gervase's name left no mistake of how he felt about the man who had hired Nell.

"Oh, Allegra! Allegra!" cried Felicity. "Everything belongs to Allegra! This house, the stables, the horses—"

"Yes, and you better believe it. There is no way to break a will; that is, unless—" Desmond halted. "Only in the event of Allegra's death would the entire estate come to me."

"She might as well be dead." Felicity's voice was sullen, and there was a hopelessness in her words. "Lying up there day after day with no interest in life."

"Be that as it may, dear," Mrs. Selkirk said tremulously, "your father is in desperate circumstances, and we all must—"

"That's enough, Millicent. I'll attend to this. Now, look here, Felicity. Be sensible. You could do far worse. Thomas Lewis is a fine young man from an honorable family—"

"You mean a wealthy family," interrupted Felicity.

"And what's wrong with that? Money is important. *You* should know; you spend enough of it," her father accused.

"But I don't love him." Felicity's voice was now a wail.

"Love has nothing to do with it!" shouted Mr. Selkirk. "I'll have no more of this nonsense. That young man is besotted with you. He has already hinted a marriage settlement will be enormous. He is the heir of a childless uncle besides having an inheritance from his grandparents. And you will have everything you could possibly imagine or wish for—a large home, a carriage, horses of your own, a more than generous allowance—"

"And I shall be miserable."

"Better to be miserable and have a rich husband than to be poor and have your father in debtors prison," was Selkirk's heartless reply.

The bitterness in his voice along with the shocking reality that the Selkirks were in dire financial straits left Nell numb. She had not guessed that in this house where luxury and extravagance were so lavishly displayed the threat of ruin hovered. She had assumed Desmond Selkirk was an affluent businessman in his own right. To discover that he envied his niece's fortune and resented his brother's will was a stunning revelation.

If the Selkirks knew she had overheard their intimate conversation, it would be a disaster.

Sick with fear that one of them might suddenly come out and find her there in the hall, Nell eased herself out of the alcove. Darting a quick glance into the room where all of the Selkirks were turned from the door, she slipped by.

Her thoughts were turbulent. She realized that under this roof were layers and layers of secrets, subterfuge of every kind. How was one to find the truth in this labyrinth of lies?

Allegra seemed more tired than usual that evening, and Nell cut their reading session short and served her the milk and biscuits. Jewel came to help Allegra into bed, and Nell said good night and left.

As Nell got ready for bed, her thoughts dwelled on the two conversations to which she had been an unwilling listener. She could not help feeling sorry for Felicity. To be put on the block, so to speak, offered to the highest bidder, was barbaric. No better than a slave auction. Nell suppressed a shudder.

Not that Thomas Lewis was so terrible a potential husband. She recalled that morning Thomas had greeted Mr. Selkirk outside church. He seemed gentle, intelligent, pleasant. Handsome, too, although, in Nell's opinion, not as handsome as his older brother.

The thought of Hamilton Lewis came, and Nell remembered the time he had sought an introduction to her and the times she had encountered him in the village. She had been struck by his unpretentiousness and his sensitivity in helping her choose the cribbage game and suggesting the travel book for Allegra.

For Felicity's sake, Nell hoped if Thomas possessed some of Hamilton's traits and qualities, the arranged marriage would not be such a bad thing.

But then, of course, Nell knew Felicity's strong, passionate feelings lay elsewhere. Such a marriage could only mean penal servitude and lost happiness.

Nell was thankful she was not in a position where such arrangements were not only routine but accepted. She would never settle for anything like that. Nothing less than total devotion and love, if that would ever come to her. How that would happen Nell realized was an impossible dream.

It had been a long day, filled with much confusion. Nell felt infinitely weary, and for the first time since she had been at Hope's End, she fell right to sleep and slept through the night.

However, in the morning, she awoke gripped with a strange sense of foreboding. Gray light filled the windows over which she had forgotten to pull the curtains the night before. She got up and went over to look out. A gray mist enveloped the garden and beyond. Suddenly, Nell was filled with a strong sensation of apprehensive waiting. For what she didn't know; of what she dared not guess.

17

December 15, 1893

Preparations for the coming holiday house party are going forward full tilt. Mrs. Russell has been running around with a long list, checking that everything under her supervision is being carried out exactly. Wallis is busy assisting Jewel and the extra help that has been hired from the village. Miss Benedict is in her element as a consultant to Mrs. Selkirk, who is more flustered than ever over the dozens of things to do.

With her protective circle unusually occupied, Allegra and I are often alone. Except, of course, for Nanny, who is always present but engrossed in her handiwork— the doilies and antimacassars she diligently crochets. But she is so hard of hearing that even if Allegra were talking she wouldn't overhear.

The wonderful thing is that Allegra and Carrick are corresponding regularly. I take her letters to him and leave them in a hollowed-out tree trunk near the lake, while he encloses letters to her in envelopes addressed to me. He's been writing so frequently that Miss Benedict once remarked snidely, "You must have a secret admirer, Miss Winston. You get more mail than anyone." I pay no attention.

Speaking of letters, I received one from Mr. Montgomery. In it he said he was going abroad and would be out of the country. I'm afraid our letters may have crossed in the mail and that he may not have received the one I wrote telling him some of my misgivings about Allegra's care, especially my doubts about Dr. Herbert. Perhaps it will be forwarded to him and he will reply. I am badly in need of his advice.

I am so happy that Allegra and Carrick are finding their way back to each other, in spite of Desmond Selkirk's objections. Whatever they could be. Carrick's sincerity and devotion to Allegra is evident.

The house has been decorated for Christmas, but a joyful spirit is sadly lacking. The swags of greens tied with red velvet bows above all the long windows, the scented candles placed in centers of crimson-berried holly and ivy vines draped on the mantelpieces in all the rooms, the twining of red satin ribbon between the railings of the staircase—all this has been done by servants. No one in the Selkirk family participated in any of it.

Trimming the tree, making scented candles, hanging the traditional wreath on the front door are always a *big part of the Christmas season at my aunts' home. Frugal as those ladies are, there is no skimping at this holiday. Here at Hope's End, the sacred quality of the special season has been completely overshadowed by plans for the party. It appears to be the only thing anyone is thinking about.*

It made me sad to see that Allegra has been left out of the festivities. So I decided Allegra should have a tiny tree of her own. When I brought it into her room and suggested we make ornaments for it ourselves, Allegra's eyes lit up. She entered into the activity, and we had great fun. She smiled with genuine delight when we finished. In fact, smiles seem to come more easily and often now. I hope it isn't wishful thinking but that the letters exchanged between her and Carrick may have turned the tide. She does not seem so melancholy. Maybe she is beginning to picture a brighter future. If so, I'm glad I risked bringing it about regardless of the possible consequences.

No one but Nell seemed to notice the change in Allegra. It was Felicity around whom everything circulated. Felicity came and went always in a breathless rush. She would call for the carriage, then skim down the stairway leaving a trail behind her—a forgotten scarf, a dropped glove, the fragrance of her exotic perfume. "Had it made special for her, when they was in Cologne last year," Jewel said one day to Nell. She passed on tidbits of gossip as well. Nell had the impression that Jewel resented but was also fascinated by Felicity.

Nell felt sad that Felicity's bright aura almost completely diminished Allegra. It should be Allegra attending the neighborhood holiday parties, dancing the night away at country balls. No one seemed to remember that this was really Allegra's house, that she should be the one being honored at the festive party.

Nell's feeling that Allegra was being ignored was somewhat lightened when a large package for Allegra arrived from London a few days before Christmas. Nell carried the box upstairs to Allegra's room. Upon opening it, they found a luxurious set of furs—a cossack style hat, a muff, and a cape of Russian sable. Enclosed was a card signed, "Your loving uncle, Gervase Montgomery."

"Oh, Allegra, how beautiful!" Nell exclaimed.

Allegra scribbled something on her pad and held it out to Nell. "Model it for me!"

Nell put on the hat, flung the cape around her shoulders, put her hands in the muff, and twirled around a couple of times. She had never worn anything so richly extravagant. Allegra smiled and clapped her hands. Then Nell took off the hat and playfully set it on Allegra's head; she handed her the muff and draped the fur cape around her shoulders. "Perfect!" she declared. "As soon as the weather is milder you must wear them outside." That was the first time anything had been said about Allegra going outside since the first disastrous outing.

Allegra did not look frightened at all by this remark. In fact, she smiled and smoothed the soft fur with her hands. Her expression was thoughtful. Nell hoped she might be thinking of how she would look in Carrick's eyes.

The evening before the Christmas ball, a dinner party with two dozen guests was held. The guest list consisted of a select group of neighbors, mainly members of other gentry families in the community.

Mrs. Selkirk asked Nell to come into the drawing room after dinner to play the piano for the ladies while they waited for the gentlemen, lingering at the table over brandy and cigars, to join them. Nell had her reservations about providing such a musical background for idle chatter. She was sure none of the women present would pay much attention. They would be too busy evaluating each other's dresses and jewels and indulging in gossip and trivia.

However, she had eyed the grand piano in the drawing room with longing ever since she had arrived. Taught to play by her aunt Hester when she was a little girl, Nell was grateful she had learned to appreciate music and loved to play. She had enjoyed playing during the tea hour at Seaview and so looked forward to the opportunity.

Before going downstairs, Nell went into Allegra's room to say good night. Allegra nodded approvingly, made a circling gesture with her hand to indicate Nell was to turn around to show off her gown. Then she wrote, "You'll be the most elegant one there!"

"I don't think so." Nell laughed. Her simply styled amber taffeta with the cameo brooch nestled in the ruffled lace jabot would be no match for the expensive gowns most of the Selkirks' lady guests would be wearing. "But thank you for saying so. You're a dear." She bent to kiss Allegra's cheek. As she did, Allegra took her hand and squeezed it.

Nell felt gratified as she went downstairs. She and Allegra had developed a warm friendship in spite of all those who had tried to prevent it.

Pausing in the hall, Nell felt a little daunted as she surveyed the drawing room filled with women glittering with jewels and wearing ornate gowns. Then she looked over at the piano, its lid open, its keys awaiting her touch. It had remained closed most of the time she had been here. Whether or not anyone else appreciated it, she would enjoy playing the magnificent instrument.

As soon as she began to play, a lovely concentration came over Nell. She no longer cared if anyone was listening. She was startled when a deep, male voice said, "You play beautifully." Looking up, she saw Hamilton Lewis standing in the curve of the piano. Splendid in evening clothes, he looked more handsome than ever—dark, wavy hair, kind, gray-blue eyes, fine white teeth.

"May I?" he asked. Smiling, he leaned slightly forward, his hand outstretched to turn the music sheets for her.

Until he spoke, Nell had not been aware the gentlemen had rejoined the ladies. Farnsworth and Lawrence began setting up card tables for whist and bridge. Nell lifted her hands from the keyboard.

"Don't stop." Hamilton put up his hand to prevent her from closing the lid.

"I must. They are getting ready to play cards. They'll want you for bridge."

"I detest bridge. I'd much rather listen to you play or simply talk with you. You can't leave now."

Nell hesitated. She glanced toward Mrs. Selkirk, who was too preoccupied to notice them. The tables were filled and cards were being dealt. As if reading her thoughts, Hamilton said, "See, we won't be missed." He smiled and led her over to a curved loveseat a little apart from the other guests, and they sat down.

Hamilton asked about Allegra and seemed pleased when Nell replied, "She seems much better. Thanks to some of your suggestions, she seems livelier, taking more pleasure in things."

"How could she not with you as a companion?"

Nell felt warmth rise into her cheeks at his compliment. To divert attention from herself, she quickly said, "The travel book was a wonderful idea. She has become totally engrossed in planning a dream trip."

"I'm planning a dream trip of my own. One I mean to put into reality," Hamilton said. "To Egypt. Have you read about the amazing archaeological discoveries that were made there in 1887? I am fascinated with that whole region. I want to take at least a year to travel and explore Egypt, take a steamer down the Nile."

Luckily, Nell had read of some of the things Hamilton talked about with such great enthusiasm. There was enormous interest in England about the recent discoveries in

Egypt—all things Egyptian. Nell had always been intrigued by the stories of the pharoahs' tombs and the treasures they contained.

As they talked, Nell lost track of time until she caught Mrs. Selkirk's curious glance. She noticed the servants were now bringing in refreshments. An hour must have passed. Realizing she had overstayed her allotted time among the Selkirks' guests, she stood and said to Hamilton, "This has been a most enjoyable discussion, but I must really excuse myself."

The light in his eyes dimmed immediately. "Must you?"

Afraid she might show how much she would like to stay, Nell murmured, "Yes. Good night, Mr. Lewis."

"*Hamilton*, please, Miss Winston."

She took a long breath but just nodded and left.

It was hard for Nell to settle down for the night. Flights of fancy kept her awake. Her always vivid imagination pictured other possibilities, other times, places she and Hamilton might have met without the social barriers of her present circumstances. What if they had met on a walking tour in the Lake country or on a ship going to Egypt? She fantasized them viewing the pyramids or the sphinx. . . . Nell didn't remember finally drifting off.

18

I have the most marvelous idea. I just hope I can bring it about. This morning, after breakfast, I peeked into the drawing room and found it transformed. Tasseled gold ropes drape the door frames and ceiling, and streamers of red satin ribbons hang from the crystal chandeliers. Large bouquets of red roses in silver vases grace tables under the baroque mirrors between each garlanded window all around the room.

A dais has been built for the orchestra that will provide dance music for the ball. I can imagine couples spinning around the big room to the melodies, the ladies in colorful gowns, the men in swallow-tailed evening clothes. As I looked around, I spotted the balcony at one end, something I'd never noticed before. In old homes this was called a minstrels' gallery, a place where the musicians would play. That is when I got my idea. Why couldn't Allegra attend the party? Concealed

from sight in the gallery, Allegra could watch the whole
panorama. Now all I have to do is convince her.

The ball was to begin at nine o'clock. Nell decided to wait
until after Wallis had taken away Allegra's supper tray to suggest it to Allegra. That way Allegra would not have too much
time to think about it and change her mind. The element of
surprise was important.

When Nell went to Allegra's room, she found Allegra alone,
except for Nanny. It seemed Miss Benedict had gone into the
village, and Wallis was helping out downstairs. Seeing her
chance, Nell launched right into her plan.

"Allegra, wouldn't you like to go to the party?"

Allegra looked startled.

"We could sit in the minstrels' gallery overlooking the
ballroom and hear the music and watch the dancing.
Wouldn't you enjoy that?" Nell made her voice as enthusi-
astic as possible.

A glimmer of excitement flickered in Allegra's eyes, then
almost immediately she shook her head.

"But why not?" asked Nell. "You wouldn't have to see anyone if you didn't want to. We would be quite out of sight up
there, and we could see everything. It would be ever so much
fun."

Allegra grabbed her pad; scribbling something quickly,
she held it out. "*You* can go."

This time Nell shook her head. "Not without you," she declared. "But I would like to go, so please won't you consider it?"

Allegra tipped her head to one side as if considering it.

"It would be such a treat to get dressed up. I'll help you
pick something, and I'll do your hair; I'm quite good at that."
Nell chattered on gaily hoping her own enthusiasm would
be contagious. She walked over to the armoire and opened
the double doors.

It was filled with beautiful clothes. Why shouldn't it be?

Allegra had just turned eighteen when the accident happened, on the brink of entering into society. Jewel had told Nell a huge debut party had been planned, to be given by Allegra's parents. Like all young ladies of her class and social station, Allegra was to be introduced to the small elite world into which she would move and from whom she would choose a suitor and eventually a husband.

What a pity, Nell thought as she sifted through the gowns. Most of them looked as though they had never been worn and were still veiled in muslin dust cloths to protect the delicate lace, sumptuous satin, lustrous silk, and soft velvet materials.

Dreams were and always had been Nell's own escape from the humdrum. If she could only entice Allegra to dream, to imagine a life of freedom again, a life where she could love and be loved. Nell knew she must try.

There was no reason Allegra could not look every bit as beautiful now with the right color to bring out her soft eyes, her lovely hair, her rare smile—a smile that Nell was determined to tempt. She whirled around and asked, "Which one will it be, Allegra?"

Nanny looked up from her chair where she was taking the contents out of the big, cretonne bag she carried with her at all times. The bag contained an odd assortment of items: a bag of lemon drops, balls of twine, tattered religious tracts, a pair of scissors, spectacles, an extra crochet hook, a ring of keys. Nanny was constantly digging in it, trying to find something. Now, however, her attention was focused on Nell as she brought out one lovely gown after the other, holding them up for Allegra to choose. Nell noticed Nanny was grinning and nodding her approval.

"Please, Allegra, do say yes," Nell pleaded.

For a few seconds, a shadow passed over Allegra's face as if she were remembering how her life had once been. Music, parties, romance. As Allegra hesitated, Nell prayed. If only

Nell could get her to dream again, to imagine the possibilities of what life could hold for her and perhaps for Carrick.

All at once Allegra smiled; her eyes took on a sparkle Nell had not seen in them before. She'd won! Allegra had agreed. Nell asked again, "Which dress will it be, Allegra?"

All the gowns were gorgeous, the most exquisite array Nell had ever seen. At last she and Allegra decided on a shimmering golden satin with a portrait neckline and puffed sleeves that tapered to the wrist.

"Jewelry?"

Allegra pointed to a mahogany chest then to which drawer Nell should open. It was the top one and completely lined with gray velvet and filled with lovely pieces of jewelry. Dazzled, Nell drew out a gold chain with an oval opal pendant and matching earrings. "These?" Allegra nodded excitedly.

"Now your hair," Nell said. She brushed and swirled Allegra's wavy hair into a loose knot and secured it with a lovely gold hair ornament she had found in the jewelry drawer.

At just that moment Wallis came in the room. She looked at Allegra, at the open armoire, back to Allegra and then at Nell, her expression aghast.

Nell, hairbrush still in hand, said in as calm a voice as she could manage, "Allegra's going to the ball, Wallis."

"Well, I never—" For once Wallis seemed to be at a loss for words. She went over and picked up the dresses Nell and Allegra had rejected and hung them back in the closet. "Does Mrs. Selkirk know about this?" she asked Nell.

Nell simply shook her head, then stood back to survey Allegra's hair.

Wallis emitted several "Tsk-tsks" but said nothing more.

"Wallis, please go and ask Lawrence to come up; we need him to carry Miss Allegra to the minstrels' gallery. There she'll be able to see everything that goes on."

At first Nell was afraid Wallis was going to refuse. Wallis cast a sharp look at Allegra and in that split second evidently decided this would be beneficial. She pursed her mouth, then gave Nell a brisk nod and went out of the room.

Nell's heart was beating uncomfortably fast; she had taken a large risk. Taking a long breath to steady herself, she reached out to Allegra and took her hand. Allegra squeezed Nell's hand and smiled.

Nanny struggled up from her chair by the fireplace and said in her wavering voice, "Oh, my dear child, if you don't look a picture of your precious mama." The smile on the wrinkled face and the faded eyes briefly brightened with tears gave Nell the reassurance she needed.

Wallis returned with Lawrence, and Nell helped them get Allegra into the wheelchair. Still a bit unsure of her plan, Nell prayed, *Please, Lord, let me not have made a mistake.*

The musicians were tuning their instruments as Lawrence carried Allegra into the minstrels' gallery. Nell and Lawrence settled Allegra comfortably in an armchair and angled it so she was hidden by the velvet draperies but had a good view of everything below. Wallis remained well in the background; evidently she was not willing to trust Nell completely with the care of Allegra.

Nell hurried back to her own room and dressed quickly, afraid something might happen to change Allegra's mind. Remembering the pair of small opera glasses she had, Nell opened her bureau drawer to look for them. It would be amusing to pass them back and forth with Allegra as they picked out different guests and vignettes taking place at the ball. After a quick search, she found them and hurried back along the hallway to rejoin Allegra.

A lilting waltz was playing as Nell took a seat beside Allegra. She noticed with happy relief that Allegra was smiling and her fingers were moving on the arm of her chair, tapping out the melody. She was enjoying herself. Satisfied that her idea had been a good one, Nell put the glasses to her eyes and scanned the ballroom below. The dance floor was filling up with circling waltzers. She was looking for the

Lewis brothers. Hamilton was nowhere to be seen among the dancers, but Thomas Lewis was hovering adoringly over Felicity.

Felicity was undoubtedly the most spectacular young woman at the ball. Her gown was a deep rose *peau du soie* that showed off her plump white shoulders and tiny waist. Stiffened ruffles of lace formed short cap sleeves, and a band of tiny pink roses wreathed her golden chignon. Rose topaz pendant earrings sparkled as she moved her head in animated chatter with three other young men who surrounded her. She furled and unfurled her fan flirtaciously at each one, laughing gaily. *The consummate actress,* Nell thought, half-amused. What lay behind the bright smile, the laughter?

As one of Felicity's admirers whirled her out to dance, Nell surveyed the room and finally found the person for whom she was searching. Hamilton Lewis was conversing with another gentleman. Nell's heart quickened. She felt a warm glow remembering their conversation the night before. How charming he had been; she would dearly love to spend more time with him, exploring other avenues of mutual interest. She knew he was well-read and interested in a myriad of subjects. She sighed.

Nell kept the opera glasses on him while her mind wandered in an imaginary interview: *What are your dreams? Who are your heroes? Who are your favorite authors? Do you like poetry as well as history? What makes—*

Nell's mental meandering was brought to a sharp halt by Allegra's sudden intake of breath. It was more a gasp, the sound of someone deeply shocked. Nell took the glasses down and turned quickly to her. Allegra had turned white; her hands were clenched and pressed to her mouth. Nell was beside her in a second.

"What is it, Allegra? What's wrong?"

Allegra looked at Nell; tears welled up in her eyes and her mouth opened as if she were desperately trying to tell her something. Allegra pointed down to the ballroom. Nell leaned over the balcony just in time to see Carrick Rowe in a heated confrontation with Desmond Selkirk. Desmond had taken Carrick's arm and was trying to move him through the doorway out of the ballroom, but Carrick was resisting. People nearby began turning their heads to stare.

Nell glanced back at Allegra. "Did you know he planned to come?"

Allegra shook her head no.

Wallis, now aware that something was wrong, moved quickly to Allegra and asked anxiously, "What's the matter, love?"

Nell had never heard Wallis speak so tenderly. Allegra turned to her, sobbing, and Wallis put her arms around her, glaring over Allegra's head at Nell. "See? Look what's happened here. She's all upset, and what for? For nothin' but to make you feel important that you got her to do something no one else could. Now see what you've done."

Nell could almost understand Wallis's anger. *But this isn't my fault,* Nell wanted to say. She could not have foreseen Carrick crossing over the line the Selkirks had drawn for him. He had probably decided "faint heart ne'er won fair lady" and literally leapt over the wall to be with her. He must have planned to make his way upstairs to see Allegra while the party was going on. Invitations were shown at the door and collected by Farnsworth upon guests' arrival, but Carrick must have maneuvered past the butler, then been seen by Selkirk, who tried to stop him.

Nell looked over the balcony rail again and saw that Selkirk, with the help of Dr. Herbert and another man, had managed to shove Carrick from the ballroom, out of the sight of the other guests. Nell turned her attention to Allegra.

"It will be all right, Allegra, I'm sure," she said, hoping that her words of assurance were true.

Allegra kept shaking her head, tears flowing. Suddenly the door to the minstrels' gallery burst open and Carrick rushed in. He must have escaped his would-be captors, dashed up the stairway, and run straight down the hall to the door opening into the balcony. He was on his knees beside Allegra, his arms around her waist. He was breathless but managed to say her name over and over. But only for a mere minute. On his heels came a puffing, red-faced Desmond, followed by Colin Herbert, pale but livid, and Lawrence.

"Get out of here!" Desmond shouted at Carrick. He waved in Lawrence and another footman and ordered, "Get this scoundrel out of here! See that he is out of this house and doesn't get back in!" Desmond shook his fist at Carrick. "I should call the sheriff on you! Trespassing, that's what you were doing. Now, get out!"

Arms flailing, legs kicking, Carrick was dragged away, protesting at the top of his voice. By this time Allegra was hysterical. Wallis was doing her best to soothe her. She kept stroking her hair, holding her, patting her back while Nell stood helplessly by.

Dr. Herbert whirled around and asked in a steely voice, "Whose idea was this?"

Wallis's gaze went accusingly to Nell.

Dr. Herbert's jaw clenched. "I thought as much. Now, let us get Allegra out of here and calmed down." He leaned forward as if to lift Allegra, but she shrank back, clinging to Wallis. Dr. Herbert frowned but stepped away.

Nell went to Allegra, took one of her trembling hands in her own. She felt the thin fingers tighten. At that moment, Lawrence reappeared, flushed and breathing hard, to report Carrick had been successfully evicted.

"Good." Desmond gave a brief nod, then directed him, "We must get Miss Allegra back to her room."

"Yes, sir." Quickly Lawrence went to Allegra's side and gently picked her up. He carried her out of the gallery down the hall with all the rest following.

At the door to Allegra's suite, Dr. Herbert turned and said to Mr. Selkirk, "Wallis and I can handle this, Desmond. I'll give her something to calm her down. No need for you to come." Then his cold eyes pierced Nell. "You won't be needed either, Miss Winston."

Nell started to object, but his icy demeanor stopped her words before she could utter them. Mr. Selkirk halted, his girth blocking her way, yet behind him she could see Dr. Herbert take a small bottle containing a clear, gray liquid, which he poured into a small tumbler. Nell saw Allegra wince, draw back, averting her head as if in refusal. "Now be a good girl, Allegra," Dr. Herbert said, "if you know what's best for you . . ." His tone was soft, but underneath was an edge of steel that chilled Nell. There was nothing she could do but helplessly watch as the doctor guided the glass firmly to Allegra's lips. Sickened, Nell turned away. As she walked back to her room, she could not forget the panic in Allegra's eyes.

She had almost reached her bedroom when she saw Miss Benedict hurrying down the hallway. She was dressed for the party in a gown that was enough out of style for Nell to notice and of a bottle green color that clashed with her newly hennaed hair. Her heavily powdered face and rouged cheeks almost made her resemble a clown. Her face was contorted now as passing Nell, she hissed, "Trouble! That's all you've done since the day you got here is cause trouble." Then she swept by in a rustle of taffeta toward Allegra's suite.

Disheartened and depressed, Nell went into her bedroom. Maybe Clarise Benedict was right. Nothing she had done in an effort to help Allegra had worked out right. Even this night that she hoped would be such a triumph had ended in disaster.

The faint sound of music playing downstairs wafted up, making her more disconsolate. She had wanted it to be such a happy occasion for Allegra, and now this. Nell sighed deeply. If it were not for the fact that Gervase Montgomery had entrusted her as Allegra's protector, she would have felt like giving up what appeared to be a futile endeavor. But he could not be reached, and she must keep her promise no matter how powerful were the forces against her efforts. Of course, she would be blamed, but that seemed unimportant now. Nell realized for the first time how truly committed she was to Allegra Selkirk.

Suddenly there was a rattling sound. She stiffened. Then it came again. Pebbles tossed against her windowpane. Nell rushed to the window and opened it.

"Miss Winston." She heard a hushed voice she recognized.

"Carrick, what are you doing? Don't you know Mr. Selkirk threatened to call the sheriff?"

"I don't care about that. I don't care what he does. He can't keep me from trying to see Allegra. Please, Miss Winston, tell her, no matter what, I'm not giving up. You will do that, won't you? You're the only one who has Allegra's true interest at heart. And mine."

"But, Carrick, I—what can I do?"

"Be her friend. She needs one desperately in this house."

Nell started to say something else, but Carrick rushed on. "Come to the dock tomorrow at three; I must know how she is, what they've done to her."

His words chilled her. "But, Carrick—"

"Please." His voice was desperate. "Promise?"

"I'll—" she started, but Carrick was gone.

Nell looked down into the dark garden and was overwhelmed with sympathy for Carrick and his fondness for Allegra. But if Desmond Selkirk decided to send her away, there would be nothing she could do.

Suddenly, she felt a tingling all through her body. In the murky dark below she saw a shape—a dim white outline that could be a man's dress shirt and a small bright glow that could be the tip of a cigar.

A guest who had wandered out from the heat of the ballroom to enjoy a quiet smoke and some fresh air on the terrace? Who? And had he overheard the conversation between her and Carrick Rowe? And if he had, what would he do with the information?

19

First thing the next morning, before going downstairs, Nell stopped by Allegra's suite, tapped quietly at the door. A haggard-looking Wallis opened it, and Nell guessed she must have kept an all-night vigil at Allegra's bedside. When she saw Nell, her face became rigid.

"Miss Allegra is sleeping; I don't intend to disturb her," she said, and she started to close the door.

"Wait, please; don't you know I feel as bad about what happened last evening as anyone? I had not the slightest hint that—"

"No matter, the harm's done," Wallis retorted. "Dr. Herbert was angry, you know. He left strict orders that Miss Allegra be let sleep until she awakened naturally."

But she had been put to sleep unnaturally, Nell almost argued. Allegra had not been allowed to deal with the emotional reaction to seeing Carrick after their long separation. Any woman would have reacted much the same. Of course, Nell said none of this. It would have been of no use. Wallis was adamant in following Dr. Herbert's instructions.

"Well, when she does awaken, please tell her I am very anxious to see her and please send me word when—"

Nell faced a closed door. She hoped Wallis would do what she requested, but she couldn't be sure.

There seemed nothing else Nell could do.

She did still have her meeting with Carrick ahead though. She was not looking forward to what she had to report to him. He was already distraught. Before she reached the dock, she saw him pacing back and forth. He turned to her eagerly. His face was drawn, his eyes circled. He probably had not slept. All she could tell him was that Allegra was resting and she had not been allowed to see her. He looked depressed. Then his demeanor underwent a change. A resolute expression took the place of the downhearted one. "Gervase should know what's going on. Have you heard from him recently?"

"He's gone abroad," Nell told him sadly. "I did write about some of my observations, but there's been no reply."

"There has to be some way . . ." He left the rest of his thought unfinished. Nell could offer no comfort. Finally, with nothing more to say to each other, they parted.

When Nell returned to the house, she was told Allegra was still sleeping. The Selkirks and Felicity had gone out for the evening. She was told Miss Benedict was with Allegra, so she had her supper alone in her room. When Jewel brought up her tray, she had her own comment on the unfortunate incident at the ball.

"Quite a hullabaloo the other night, weren't there? 'Tis a real shame. Them two have loved each other since they wuz playmates as youngsters. Carrick used to have the run of the house when the other Selkirks were alive. To think of him being forbid to come here anymore . . ." Jewel shook her head. "Thrown out like a common beggar." There was no mistaking how the maid felt about the situation.

Nell made no comment, and Jewel left. The maid's statement answered a question Nell had been turning over in her mind since that evening's fiasco. How had Carrick known about the minstrels' gallery? How did he know the way up there? Or that Allegra might be there?

They had probably played there as children. Perhaps he had been on his way to Allegra's suite when he saw her through the open door of the hallway.

The biggest question was why Desmond Selkirk was so opposed to the romance. Given his financial dilemma, perhaps he worried if they married, Carrick would then be in charge of Allegra's fortune. The law held that a married woman's property automatically belonged to her husband. Was Desmond in line to inherit Hope's End—mansion, grounds, and tenant farms? Slowly the answer came—if Allegra was dead. Only then would the younger brother fall heir to the magnificent estate. Nell shivered. The thoughts that followed were too dreadful to contemplate.

On the second morning after the unfortunate incident with Carrick, Nell again tried to see Allegra. This time she was told Allegra had been awake several times but had gone back to sleep. "I will let you know when you can see her," Wallis said firmly. "Dr. Herbert says sleep is the best thing for her right now."

There was something wrong about this, Nell thought. Somehow Dr. Herbert did not want her to be with Allegra, influence her in any way. His orders must have specifically stated that she was not to be admitted. Was he backing up Mr. Selkirk, or was it the other way around?

More than anything, Nell worried that the sedative he administered must have been very, very strong. Too strong for someone as frail as Allegra, Nell was convinced. But what could she do about it?

Turned away again from seeing Allegra, Nell decided she must get in touch with Gervase. Surely he had left a forwarding address at his club and eventually her letter would reach him. She went to her room, sat down at the desk, and brought out her stationery. Her pen flew across the paper then stopped. She had written critically of Dr. Herbert,

Desmond, and also of the attitudes of Miss Benedict and Wallis toward her. She could understand Wallis's protective instinct. But Clarise Benedict? Why is she so resentful? All Nell had done was try to help Allegra regain her zest for life in ways no one else had tried. What lay behind all that hostility? A brutal childhood, a loveless womanhood, fear of a lonely old age? Afraid of being pushed out into an uncaring world where old people are considered useless, unwanted?

Reading over what she had written, Nell wondered if it was too emotional for a letter to Gervase. Maybe it sounded irrational? Perhaps she should simply say that she was concerned about Allegra's situation and did not see how improvement was possible if things continued as they were.

After several false starts, which landed in the wastebasket, Nell finally completed a short note, closing with, "If it would be possible, I would like to meet with you and discuss this in person. I could come up to London, or perhaps we could meet at some midway point."

Satisfied that the tone of the letter was reasonable, Nell folded it, then put it in an envelope on which she wrote his name and the address he had given her. Not wanting to place it on the hall table with other outgoing mail, Nell decided she would walk into the village and mail the letter herself at the post office.

She dressed warmly, for it was a cold, blustery winter day, and it would be a long walk to the village and back.

At the post office, she mailed her letter. The day had turned bitterly cold, and she had no inclination to shop or even go into the cheerful tearoom. For some reason, she felt a strange urgency to get back to the house that seemed so unwelcoming to her.

Back at the house, she hurried upstairs. Reaching the top of the stairs, Nell decided to go to Allegra's room to see how she was. This time she was determined not to be refused admission.

Wallis was still in attendance, but she made no excuse,

and Nell went in. Allegra was not in her wheelchair but lying on the lounge in front of the fireplace. She turned her head as Nell came in, and a faint smile lifted the corners of her mouth. Nell came close, bent down, and gazed into Allegra's eyes. She looked as if she had been crying. The expression on her face, forlorn, wretched, went straight to Nell's heart. Impulsively, she put her cool cheek against Allegra's. She wanted to comfort her, but she wasn't sure she had gained Allegra's full confidence yet. Something deep, deeper than Nell could imagine, was troubling the young woman. How could she help unless she knew what it was?

Allegra's eyes filled with tears turning them into glistening black pearls. "What is it, Allegra? Can you tell me?" Nell whispered.

She had hardly gotten the words out when the door opened and Clarise Benedict came into the room. Her sudden appearance startled both Nell and Allegra.

Allegra barely controlled a look of distaste.

"Dr. Herbert is talking with your uncle now, but he'll be up here himself in a few minutes to see how you are." Miss Benedict's voice was as smooth as silk.

At the mention of Dr. Herbert, Nell saw a shadow come over Allegra's face. Was she frightened of the doctor or some new treatment he was giving her?

Miss Benedict fussed about, making a great show of tidying things up. While she was thus occupied, Allegra grabbed her pad, scribbled something on it, tore it off, crushed it into Nell's hand, then put her forefinger up to her lips. A moment later the door opened and Dr. Herbert entered the room. Seeing Nell, his face underwent a quick change. He regarded her with an intimidating stare, then gave her a mocking smile.

"Excuse us, if you will, Miss Winston; this is a professional visit."

Nell bent down and whispered to Allegra, "I'll be back

later." Then she got up and left the room without looking at either the doctor or Clarise.

In the hallway under one of the wall lamps, Nell uncrumpled the slip of paper Allegra had thrust into her hand and read what the young girl had written in such haste: "He wants me to go to a private sanitarium." Who was *he?* Her uncle or Dr. Herbert? Who did Allegra mean?

Nell walked slowly down the hall to her room, turning everything over in her mind—the scribbled note, Allegra's troubled demeanor, and what it all meant. She must find out. It did seem as though at last Allegra was reaching out for help. Whatever it cost, Nell intended to give it.

The minute she opened the door to her room, she felt something was amiss. A kind of sick dismay coursed through her as a strong sensation took hold. Someone had been in there. Her gaze swept over the room. The conviction grew. Objects slightly moved, a drawer not quite closed, the armoire door slightly ajar. Someone with a purpose had been here going through her things.

Anger now replaced her first feelings of bewilderment. Nell moved quickly around the room; she went to her armoire and rapidly checked her meager wardrobe. Her bonnets hadn't been moved, her boots and shoes were all lined up neatly. She went to her dressing table; she owned nothing of real value. However, she opened her small jewel box. Her cameo brooch, pearl stud earrings, and seed pearl necklace were untouched. She was wearing her pendant watch and gold heart earrings, which were her only other jewelry. Nothing missing. So what would anyone be searching for? What did Nell have that would be of importance to anyone else?

Then she thought of her journal. Did someone know about it? With a guilty start, she thought of all the frank comments she had made about every member of the household. She thought too of the personal comments about Allegra's condition and her lack of progress. Anyone who got a peek inside that journal would get a look into her mind. It was a dreadful invasion of privacy.

She opened the desk drawer. The journal was in place just where she had put it after the last time she had written in it. Then her eye caught something else. The small stack of letters she had received since her arrival.

She picked up the sheaf of envelopes and sifted through them; there were several from both aunts, a few from a school friend she had kept in touch with all these years. Then she saw the one from Gervase Montgomery, the one saying he was going abroad, the letter Nell felt had crossed hers right before Christmas.

Was this where it had been in the sequence of the letters? Or had it been pulled out from the rest and read? She couldn't tell, couldn't know. But if it had . . .

She took it out of the envelope now and reread it.

> My dear Miss Winston,
> I am sure by now you may have had second thoughts about accepting the task I have given you. Perhaps you have found the situation at Hope's End much different and much worse than I had described, but if you are the woman of intelligence, perception, and compassion I took you to be, you will soon know what to do to help my niece.
> You must be diligent, observant, discerning, and if you see any way I can possibly find just cause to assert my prerogative as guardian of Allegra and remove her from the influences I feel are detrimental to her well-being, you are to notify me immediately so I can take action.
> You may reach me at my London club until the first of the year when I shall be abroad traveling for a time so will have no permanent address.
> Yours very sincerely,
> Gervase Montgomery

How would anyone else interpret this letter? What hidden messages would they find between the lines? Surely one conclusion would be that Nell had been sent here as a spy to indict the combined household of negligence or mismanagement of the life of Allegra Selkirk. No wonder she had been under suspicion from the beginning. Finding this letter would only confirm them. But who had been the reader?

Nell put the letter back in with the others and shut the desk drawer; she remained sitting there, stunned with her discovery. Whoever had read her personal journal now knew her doubts about the goodwill and the motives of each member of the household. That fact, coupled with the information that Gervase would be out of touch for an indefinite period of time, left Nell feeling terribly vulnerable and threatened.

A slow burning fury took over Nell's first reaction to having her room searched. Even the wastebasket beside the desk with its batch of discarded half-written letters to Gervase had been riffled through, Nell could tell. Who had been the invader? And for what purpose? For what were they searching? Some evidence that they could use against her?

Although shaken, Nell's concern was mainly for Allegra. If someone was trying to get rid of her, it would remove Allegra's last defense. Except for Carrick and Gervase, Nell was the only one who really wanted Allegra well. Without that hope, she felt Allegra's spirit would be destroyed.

Composing herself, Nell left her room and went down the hall to Allegra's. She was determined to see her no matter how Wallis resisted. However, Wallis opened the door to Nell's knock. When she entered, she was relieved to see Miss Benedict was not there, only Nanny drowsing by the fireplace. Nell moved quickly to Allegra's lounge but found her lethargic. Allegra turned her head listlessly at Nell's approach, her eyes heavy-lidded and dull. She must still be under the effects of the sedative Dr. Herbert had given her. It must be very strong indeed. Had it really been necessary?

Leaning closer, Nell saw that her pupils were quite dilated. Something was dreadfully wrong, Nell knew. Alarmed and concerned, she drew up a chair and sat down, taking one of Allegra's limp hands in her own. Allegra stared at Nell languidly as if she had no strength to try to communicate. Her eyelids fluttered as if it were an effort to keep them open. Gradually they closed, but Nell remained there, holding Allegra's hand.

She wasn't sure how long she'd been sitting there when a tap on her shoulder caused her to turn. Wallis stood there holding Tippy's leash indicating that he had not been taken out for his daily run. Nell nodded. She hated leaving Allegra. But she felt sorry for the little dog cooped up all day in the stuffy rooms, and it was her duty to walk Tippy. Besides, it looked as though Allegra would probably sleep for a long time.

Not taking time to go back to her room for her coat, Nell decided she could wear the ulster that hung at the garden door. But just as she entered the room, she nearly collided with Felicity, who was wearing the ulster and was just coming in from outside. Her hair was wind-tossed, damp tendrils of curls clung to her rosy cheeks, and her lips had that softness Nell had noted before.

For a moment the two stared at each other. A few rapid changes of expression passed over Felicity's face. She seemed to be trying to decide whether to explain where she was returning from or make some other excuse. Then the moment passed, and she chose to do neither. She lifted her chin defiantly then slung the ulster back on its hook and swept past Nell without saying anything. Nell knew anyway. It was obvious Felicity, in spite of her father, was continuing her romance with Hugh Douglass. How long could the two maintain this secret?

Well, it was no business of hers, Nell told herself. She had more troubling problems on her mind. She got down the ulster, wrapped herself in it, and went outside. It was already getting dark, and the wind was cold. Tippy tugged at the leash. Now that he was accustomed to their routine, she would unhook it and let him go free. He scampered off, and Nell followed along the gravel walkways. She felt depressed about Allegra's condition. Was Dr. Herbert right that she had had too "great expectations" for her recovery? Had Gervase been too gullible, too ready to accept Dr. Freud's new theories? Had she overstepped herself by encouraging Carrick? Nell shuddered and pulled the ulster tighter around her shivering shoulders. It had really grown dark now and, looking back at the house, Nell saw lights in the windows. Soon it would be the dinner hour, and she would have to go down and face all those people, one of whom she suspected had invaded her privacy, surreptitiously read her journal, her letters. It almost sickened Nell to imagine it. She felt chilled.

It was getting cold; she stamped her feet and whistled for Tippy. Where was the little scamp? She called again and he came racing along the path, panting as he ran. She snapped the leash back on his collar and went inside.

Dinner was more strained than ever that evening. Nell could hardly bear to look at anyone knowing her gaze might be accusatory. She was glad when dessert was served and she could excuse herself.

After a brief visit to Allegra's room, where she found Wallis settling her into bed, Nell went to her own. She felt weighed down with the accumulated questions that whirled in her mind. She went over and over the events one by one but they remained unresolved. Preoccupied, she prepared for bed, then picked up her Bible to do her nightly Scripture reading before trying to sleep.

She was now in the Book of Luke, and her marker was placed at the beginning of chapter 12. As she began to read, she was suddenly wide awake. The second and third verses read: "For there is nothing covered, that shall not be revealed;

neither hid, that shall not be known. Therefore whatsoever ye have spoken in darkness shall be heard in the light; and that which ye have spoken in the ear in closets shall be proclaimed upon the housetops."

Nell's hands gripped the edges of the book. This passage was almost identical to the one in Mark she had read the first night she had been at Hope's End.

Nell thought of all she now had learned about undercurrents lurking under the surface of the life in this household—the secrets, the whispered threats, the hidden plans.

Could this be coincidence? Or was this, like Aunt Hester always maintained, God's Word as a two-edged sword?

For some reason, the next morning Nell woke up with a new sense of purpose. She saw her role as Allegra's defender, a buffer, a ray of hope and light penetrating the darkness in which others seemed to cloak Allegra. She would do her best to carry out the goal Gervase had given her. No matter what.

Thankfully Allegra seemed more alert when Nell went in to see her. The effects of the sedative had at last worn off and she eagerly agreed to Nell's suggestion of how they could use the travel book Lady Anne Lewis had sent.

They began by planning a dream trip to Italy and started mapping out their itinerary—where they would go first, what they would see in each place, the museums, cathedrals, and castles. Allegra took to the idea enthusiastically and did not seem the least tired, nor did her interest flag. In fact, she insisted Nell have her supper on a tray along with her so they could continue their game.

In the next day's mail, Nell received a note from Carrick and a letter for Allegra. The note to Nell said, "I am working on a plan I believe will free Allegra. Could you meet me in the village day after tomorrow? By then I may have things in place. However, I will need your cooperation. Please meet me at the Buttercup at three o'clock. This is urgent."

What was Carrick up to, and had she been wrong to get

so involved in this matter? She was now in a conspiracy as secret as any in this house. She slipped Carrick's letter to Allegra during their tea time and was rewarded by a tremulous smile, a brightening of her eyes. Nell prayed she was doing the right thing.

The next two days brought a marked change in Allegra, and Nell was gratified. Even if Allegra's preference for her company caused Miss Benedict to be resentful and Wallis to wear a constant grieved expression.

On Thursday, it was with some misgivings that Nell went to the village to meet Carrick. She had to have some reason, some errand to explain going out on such a blustery winter afternoon. In the presence of both Wallis and Miss Benedict, Nell mentioned she wanted to get a birthday gift for her aunt Emma, a tapestry to work or even a puzzle such as the one she had found for Allegra.

Armed with an umbrella, Nell left soon after lunch. She walked briskly. The wind tugged at her skirt, whipped her bonnet strings.

Carrick was waiting for her at the tearoom door, and they went inside. At first he seemed calm, but the more he talked, outlining his plan, the more worried Nell became. It was a plan fraught with risk. Danger even. There could be serious legal repercussions.

"I am waiting to hear from Allegra's uncle Gervase before I proceed, of course. I have written him in care of his London club with the envelope marked *extremely urgent.*" Carrick's hand moved nervously, crumbling the scone he had ordered but did not eat. "There must be something he can do."

Nell felt uneasy. Carrick tended to be impulsive. Rash. She thought of his actions the night of the Christmas ball.

"You will help us, won't you, Miss Winston?"

"I will if—we must wait until we hear from Mr. Montgomery. Only he has the authority to act on Allegra's behalf.

What you're suggesting, Mr. Rowe, could be construed as kidnapping." The word almost stuck in her throat.

"Not if the so-called victim is willing," he replied. "I've told Allegra my plan. She'll be depending on you when the time comes."

There were still many things unresolved when Nell said she must get back to the house. Outside, on the tearoom steps, Nell looked at the sky, wondering if she would need her umbrella on the way back. Just then, to her horror, she saw Dr. Herbert's small buggy come down the street. She half turned as it passed. Had he seen them? Her heart was fluttering. She hoped not.

"I must go," she said again and started down the steps. Carrick followed. They had walked only a short way when she saw Desmond Selkirk going into The Red Fox Inn. Nell shuddered. What would Allegra's uncle think if he saw her and Carrick together?

"Would you like me to walk you back to Hope's End?" Carrick asked.

"No, thank you. That won't be necessary," Nell said quickly. Then remembering she could not go back empty-handed after making such a point of her errand, she said, "I have a few things to get at the stationer's."

Carrick put out one hand to detain her. "I know we're doing the right thing, Miss Winston."

Nell wished she felt as sure. They parted, saying they would keep in touch, and Nell went to Mr. Ives's store. Her mind was so filled with what they had discussed, the possible problems and the treacherous line she had crossed by agreeing to help Carrick, that she wandered up and down the aisles aimlessly.

The tinny ring of the bell over the door and a gust of wind brought her attention back to the present. To her astonishment, she saw the two customers entering the store were none other than Mrs. Russell and Miss Benedict. Was everyone from Hope's End in the village today? Nell's second thought was, had they seen her and Carrick? Did everyone now know she was an ally of the young man who had been banished from the house?

She quickly picked up one of the jigsaw puzzles displayed and took it to the counter. There was no way to avoid the women. She greeted them cordially.

"We were just going to the Buttercup for tea. Would you care to join us, Miss Winston?" Mrs. Russell invited.

Before she thought, Nell said, "Thank you, but I've already had tea."

The minute she spoke she realized it was a mistake. Miss Benedict's eyebrows lifted. "With a gentleman no less, Mrs. Russell." She gave Nell a sly look. "I thought that was you I saw with a gentleman on the steps of the Buttercup as we were coming down the street, but I wasn't quite sure." To Mrs. Russell she said, "I believe Miss Winston has a secret admirer."

Nell decided not to dignify Miss Benedict's mean-spirited comment with any explanation. She merely paid for the puzzle, bid them both good-bye, and left.

She was, however, worried. If she and Carrick had been seen together, it would soon be common knowledge that they were allies. Would that information be grounds for her dismissal? If that happened, what would become of Allegra?

The day's unexpected events were still very much on Nell's mind that evening. She longed to tell Allegra of her meeting with Carrick, find out how much Allegra knew and how much she was willing to go along with his plan, but there was no chance. Nanny was in her spot, Miss Benedict was settled with her knitting, and Wallis was hovering as usual.

Even Felicity stayed longer than usual when she made her visit. It was clear the cousins had little in common. However, Allegra endured the brief visits graciously.

When Wallis brought up her bedtime snack, Allegra motioned her to leave the tray, that she was not ready for it yet.

"But you always have it at half past nine, miss," Wallis protested.

Allegra didn't even look up, just shook her head.

"When she's finished, I'll take the tray back to the pantry, Wallis," Nell offered.

Wallis looked indignant. It was obvious she felt her position with Allegra was being usurped. She gave Nell a tight-lipped glare, abruptly turned, and went out of the room. Allegra, happily drawing a map of Venice, did not see the resentful vignette. Nell sighed. Anything she did was taken the wrong way. Well, it couldn't be helped. Allegra was happier than she had seen her since she'd come and that's what mattered.

It was after ten when Wallis came back and busied herself in the adjoining bedroom, turning down Allegra's bed and laying out her negligee and gown.

Not wanting to upset the maid further, Nell gently suggested to Allegra that they quit for the night. With a sigh, Allegra reluctantly agreed.

After saying good night, Nell took the tray and started down the dimly lit hall to the stairway. She was feeling particularly lighthearted, optimistic; things were going well. All of a sudden, she tripped. With a clatter, the cups, saucers, cream pitcher, and beverage pot toppled; the tray tipped, spilling everything. What was left of the milk spilled over her dress as Nell dropped the tray.

She reached out to grab the banister to keep herself from falling but lost her balance. Her hands outstretched, she plunged forward, futilely grasping for something but clutching only empty air. Her shoulders hit the wall, then she fell backward striking her head and tumbling over and over, unable to stop until she reached the bottom of the steps.

For a minute she lay there dazed, unable to move or think. She tried to raise herself but was stabbed by a wrenching pain down her arm and back. Tomorrow she would be black and blue, she thought, almost detachedly.

How had it happened? She was moving carefully, watching her step, and then . . . Nell tried to raise her head, but a sharp pain pierced her skull and everything whirled. Moaning slightly, holding on to one of the banister spokes, she pulled herself to a sitting position. She ran her hand down each leg. Nothing broken, but she felt horribly sick and dizzy.

Just then, she looked up, and in the wavery light from the lamp on the landing, she saw a face peering down at her. She struggled to make some sound, to call for help, but nothing came. A malicious smile came and went on the face so fleetingly Nell wasn't sure whether she'd really seen it. Her vision blurred. She heard voices, running feet. The face disappeared. Blackness swallowed everything. Nell closed her eyes and fell back.

Slowly, Nell opened her eyes. Dr. Herbert stood over her, an enigmatic smile on his mouth. Another face swam into view: Jewel was standing at the foot of her bed.

"How are you feeling, Miss Winston?" he asked in a quiet, professional tone.

"I don't know; I'm not sure," she murmured. "My head aches awfully . . ."

"You have a slight concussion. You took a bad fall."

"Yes, now I remember . . ." Nell's eyelids felt terribly heavy. Every bone in her body felt sore. She tried to move then moaned.

"You'll be right as rain in a day or two. Maybe a little stiff, but that's all. You were lucky. Nothing more than a badly sprained wrist."

She tried to lift her right hand but found it heavily bandaged.

"Not too high a price for being clumsy, I'd say."

Nell started to deny being clumsy. That wasn't it. But her head was pounding so she couldn't think what it was. Oh yes, she had tripped over something. Something she hadn't seen on the steps . . . a loose metal stair tread? Had her heel caught in a torn piece of carpeting? Then the image of that face peering over the banister at her—the malicious smile came thrusting forward. Had she imagined it?

She heard Dr. Herbert's voice as if from a long distance saying to Jewel, "Be sure to waken her every hour or so. Slap her cheeks lightly if she doesn't wake up right away. Help her sit up, take sips of water or strong tea. Don't let her slip into deep sleep. That could be dangerous."

Dangerous? Nell's one hand clutched the sheet. She already felt a sense of danger. But from what source she couldn't be sure. She felt too tired to explore the possibilities. Jewel was moving around the bed, bending over her. "Now you just rest, miss. I'll be back in a while," she said. Then Nell heard the door close quietly, and she was alone.

Whose face had peered at her over the banister? The light had been flickering; she could have been mistaken. Where had everyone been? The Selkirks and Felicity had gone to a party somewhere in the neighborhood. Had Miss Benedict gone too? Wallis was with Allegra, or wasn't she? Who had come to her aid? Who had found her at the bottom of the stairs? She didn't know. Who had called Dr. Herbert? Or had he already been in the house? Nell felt too weary to go on trying to think. In a little while, she'd feel better. She'd be able to sort it out then. Able to remember.

She didn't know how long she'd been asleep when she heard her bedroom door creak a little and someone move haltingly toward her bed. With an effort Nell opened her eyes and saw a wrinkled gnome of a face looking over her. A clawlike bony hand encircled her unbandaged wrist. Nanny Maybank!

Realizing Nell was awake, Nanny croaked, "I didn't mean to waken you, miss. We've been worried about you. Miss Allegra is upset about your fall. But Wallis said you weren't to be disturbed; I come to see for myself, so I can comfort Miss Allegra." She bent her wizened face closer and whispered, "How are you feeling?"

Nell wet her lips with her tongue; her throat felt dry.

"Better, I think. The doctor said I've a sprained wrist, some bruises, and that I should stay in bed for a day or so."

Nanny made a face. "The doctor, eh! I wouldn't give a twopenny for his opinion." She pulled up a straight chair and sat down beside Nell's bed. "If he's so great, why hasn't he got my girl up and on her feet and walkin' again, I ask you? I've known Colin Herbert since he was a lad, and he's always been full of himself." She folded her hands on her lap and looked around the room, then asked, "Anyone taken any of your things?"

The question startled Nell. "No."

Nanny leaned closer. "Someone's been in my room many times. Gone through my drawers. They tell me my memory's bad, and I guess it is. But certain things you know. And I know when something's missing."

Nanny was silent for a few minutes; then she said, "You're a good person; you're honest, and I can tell you love Allegra. Anyone who loves my little one, I am all for." Her faded eyes filled with tears. "It breaks my heart to see her like this. She looks so much like her dear mama, I sometimes think I'm seeing Henrietta . . . I could show you, but . . ." Her face crumpled into an expression of bewildered sadness. "Somebody took my picture of her. Of course, people tell me I'm gettin' old, forgetful, that I hide things myself then accuse them of being stolen." She shook her head and said scornfully, "I'm not that daft. It disappeared, and that's the Lord's truth."

Nanny worked her mouth, as if chewing over what she was about to relate. Her expression became thoughtful. "It was last winter when I had pleurisy, and they called the doctor to see to me. It was the first time he'd been in my room or seen the picture. It was took when Henrietta's engagement to Matthew was announced. She had several copies made. She give one to me herself. Wouldn't I treasure it then? Not do anything to misplace it or hide it? I kept it right by my bedside so I could remember her when I said my prayers at night." Her voice lowered to a hush. "But all at once it weren't there anymore. I've searched high and low for it, but I can't find it."

She cupped her mouth with one gnarled hand and whispered, "Do you think Colin took it? He was head over heels in love with her, you know. When she turned him down to marry Matthew, he went plumb crazy. I don't know that myself, but it's what I've heard."

Nell's head ached. She was losing track of what Nanny was saying. The old woman was rambling, but some of what she said registered. Fuzzy as Nell's brain felt, she still thought part of this might be true. Hadn't Lady Anne said practically the same thing about Dr. Herbert's reaction to Allegra's mother?

Nanny's voice droned on. Nell drifted off. The next thing she knew she was getting sharp little slaps on the cheeks, and Jewel's cheerful young voice with its broad Yorkshire accent was calling her name.

"Miss Winston! Wake up. Come on. I'll sit you up, and you can have a nice cup of hot tea."

Jewel plumped the pillows up behind Nell's back and held out the cup of steaming tea. "I put plenty of sugar in it to give you strength. That's what you need. You took a nasty spill." Jewel had to help Nell hold the cup as she could use only one hand.

Nell felt the warmth and sweetness flow through her. The stimulation seemed to clear her fuzziness. While Jewel went around briskly straightening the bedclothes and stoking the fire in the fireplace, Nell relived the accident. She recalled starting down the stairway, holding the tray carefully. She had stopped once to lift her dress so as not to trip on the hem or have the heel of her shoe catch on the edge of her skirt. So why had she lost her balance and fallen? Or had she been pushed?

That thought caused Nell to start, and she nearly spilled the tea. Jewel noticed and hurried to the bed. "Here, miss, let me take it. You're still not right, are you? Lie back now and try to rest." Jewel took the cup, turned up the covers, and tucked them around Nell's shivering shoulders.

Nell lay staring into space, her mind in turmoil. Try as she could, she could only go back as far as that dreadful moment when she seemed to be hurtling forward into nothingness. Some important clue was missing, but she couldn't grasp it.

"Jewel, I've been trying to figure out what made me fall. Have you noticed anything that might have caused my fall? Say, a bit of torn carpet or a metal strip on one of the steps that might have come loose? Anything that I might have tripped on?"

Jewel didn't answer right away. Nell was startled to see the change of expression on the maid's face.

Her eyes were big and round and filled with fear. She hesitated for a long minute, then put her hand in her apron pocket and drew out a long piece of twisted yarn and held it up for Nell to see.

Puzzled, Nell asked, "What's that, Jewel?"

"What do it look like, miss?" Jewel asked. Nell knew the girl wasn't trying to be flippant but was totally serious.

"Yarn, I suppose."

"I found it tied between the banister posts on the stairway where you fell the other night. Someone put it there on purpose to make you fall."

Nell felt as if someone had just dumped a bucket of ice on her, and she shuddered.

22

*N*ell had no intention of telling Allegra about what Jewel had found on the stairway; nor would she mention her own suspicions. It would just upset Allegra. Since Nell had no real foundation to go on, it was best not to say anything.

One look at Allegra and Nell felt something about her had changed. Her cheeks were flushed, her eyes bright, but not unnaturally so, as with a fever. Nell guessed it was from some inner excitement she could barely suppress. Nell sat down beside her, and Allegra reached for her hand and pressed it. Her eyes signaled she had something to tell. She had her pad of paper handy and began to write. First she wrote down several questions concerning Nell's fall and injury and expressed her sympathy. Then she hurriedly scribbled something else, tore off the page, folded it, and handed it to Nell just before Wallis came into the room.

Nell didn't have a chance to read it until later when she was alone in her own room. It had been written so quickly Allegra's usually neat handwriting looked lopsided. "Will you arrange a meeting with Carrick for me? You can take me in the wheelchair to the end of the garden. He will be waiting. He has something important to discuss with me. Please."

Nell's reaction was mixed. She was glad that Allegra was again taking control of her life. She also realized if it were discovered that *she* was responsible for reuniting the two whose romance was deemed unsuitable, she might, in spite of Gervase, be banished from Hope's End.

Whatever the risk, Allegra was depending on her. She couldn't fail her trust. Somehow she would get Allegra out of the house and down there.

Luckily, the weather took a turn for the better. A pale sun thrust its way through the morning mist, and by afternoon it was sunny with only a mild wind off the lake. Bolstered by the fact that this time Allegra wanted to go, Nell suggested the outing confidently. Wallis protested, but Nell pointed out Allegra could be bundled up well. "We'll put a blanket over her knees and a shawl around her, and she'll be snug and warm. Besides, she can wear the set of furs she received as a Christmas gift," Nell assured Wallis. Jewel was to come along to push the wheelchair since Nell's wrist was still weak.

Dressed in the Russian sable hat, muff, and cape, Allegra looked lovely. Her eyes were shining, Nell suspected, in anticipation of seeing Carrick. Whatever the cost, things must work out for the two young lovers, Nell decided. She was willing to help however she could.

Under Wallis's disapproving frown, Lawrence carried Allegra downstairs and put her in the wheelchair. Jewel took her place behind, and Nell followed with Tippy on his leash.

Just out of sight of the house, the threesome rounded the corner onto the path that led down to the lake. Almost as soon as they got there, Carrick came out from his hiding place. Discreetly, Nell and Jewel departed, each taking a separate path in the garden—Nell trying to keep up with the scampering antics of the little dog, Jewel to have a chat with the young assistant gardener.

Nell strolled leisurely down one of her favorite paths

toward the fishpond walled by a tall hawthorn hedge on either side. She felt happy, satisfied that the plan had worked out so well, when she became aware of hushed voices from the other side of the hedge. She didn't recognize the voices. Not even the gender. A man and woman? Two women? She just caught a word here and there, bits and pieces of a heated conversation.

"What do you expect?"

"I counted on you—"

"I've done all I can—"

"If you had, we'd be free."

"There's only one thing standing in our way."

"One person, you mean."

"You have to do something."

"I've no money; how can I?"

"Then I'm trapped."

"*She's* holding all the cards."

"I'm not going to wait forever."

Again Nell was caught inadvertently as an eavesdropper on a private conversation. She tugged at Tippy's leash, but the terrier was stubbornly digging at something, burrowing further under the bushes. She didn't want to pick him up and start him barking and thus reveal her presence to whoever was on the other side of the tall hedge. Finally, he backed out, and she pulled him along, hurrying back to where she had left Allegra and Carrick. As she came around the corner and caught sight of them, Allegra was in Carrick's arms, and he was kissing her tenderly. Nell halted, giving them a bit more time. At the same moment, Jewel hurried down the opposite path to join her. Carrick bid Allegra a lingering goodbye, then the three women returned to the house. Nell had never seen Allegra look so happy or so radiant.

The mail that afternoon brought a package for Nell from her aunts containing a box of Aunt Emma's special fudge and divinity. She took both along with her when she went to share tea with Allegra.

Nell could tell Allegra was happily distracted, reliving her visit with Carrick. What had they discussed? When would they come out into the open, declare their love, and refuse to allow Desmond to keep them apart any longer? If any of this had been discussed, Allegra was not sharing it. But then, Nell had secrets of her own. Underneath her surface gaiety, the twisted yarn on the steps haunted her. It was always in the back of her mind that someone had purposed to injure her, frighten her. This time their plan had been foiled. She had escaped relatively unscathed. But, would whoever planned it try again?

Allegra was enjoying herself thoroughly when Wallis came, hinting that it was time for her hot milk and bedtime. Allegra shook her head and waved her away impatiently. Unwilling to end an evening that Allegra was enjoying so much, Nell sent the maid a look she hoped was sympathetic. But Wallis left in a huff.

A while later Felicity arrived for her nightly call on Allegra. When she walked in, Nell and Allegra were laughing at something in the scrapbook they were making for their Italian dream trip. She stood, glancing from one to the other. "Well, I must say, you two look as though you're having fun!"

"You're welcome to stay," Nell said after glancing at Allegra and getting an affirmative nod.

Felicity flounced out her ruffled skirt and said with a sigh, "I'm off to a boring party. Papa would be furious if I didn't go." She made a face.

"Have a piece of fudge?" Nell held out the box, and Felicity took one. "How I envy you," she said, looking at Allegra with an unreadable expression.

Suddenly Nell felt a chill. Something about Felicity's voice struck her. Had she been one of the persons in the garden this afternoon? Snatches of what she had overheard came back into Nell's mind. "Only one thing standing in our way"; "One person, you mean"; then just now, "I envy you." Of course! Allegra was the stumbling block to Felicity's happiness. Nell also recalled the Selkirks' discussion.

"Where's Wallis?" Felicity asked, glancing around. "Doesn't she usually bring up your bedtime snack, Allegra? I passed her on the stairs, and she looked like a thundercloud."

"She may have been put out because Allegra wasn't ready for it so early."

"Want me to bring it up?"

"If you don't mind. It's probably ready; the milk just needs to be heated. Jewel may be in the pantry setting up breakfast trays; she'll show you how to use the spirit burner," Nell answered.

Returning with the tray, Felicity reported, "Wallis had it ready when I got there." She set it down beside Allegra. "Jewel was in the pantry; she showed me how to light the spirit burner and heat it." Felicity made a face. "Miss Prunes and Prisms was there too. I suspect she was snooping, as usual. Or looking for Papa's brandy!" Felicity gave a wicked little wink. Then she said, "Well, I really must go." She bent down and gave Allegra a peck on the cheek. "Good night, cousin." Turning to Nell, she said, "Good night, Miss Winston," and she rustled out, leaving a trace of exotic perfume behind.

A few minutes later, Miss Benedict came in, declaring, "My, my, it's getting very late. What are you thinking, Miss Winston, to keep Allegra up so long? Where is Wallis?" she demanded crossly. "She should be getting Allegra ready for bed." Irritated, she looked around nervously.

Almost at once, Wallis reappeared. So quickly, in fact, that Nell wondered if she had been close by and heard both Felicity and Miss Benedict asking about her.

"I was here earlier, Miss Benedict. However, Miss Winston sent me away."

Startled at this misstatement, Nell did not bother to correct her. She just gathered up the scissors and scraps and picked up the scrapbook, quietly saying, "I'm too full of cake and candy for my milk tonight, Allegra." After they exchanged an understanding look, she said good night and left, leaving Wallis and Miss Benedict with Allegra.

As soon as Nell reached her bedroom, the careful facade she had been maintaining slipped away. She suddenly felt exhausted. She got out her journal but was unable to write in it. The fact that someone might have read her intimate thoughts prohibited her from writing more. Had someone actually placed the yarn across the stairs to cause her fall, to injure her so badly she would have to leave? She felt too worn-out even to read a Bible verse. Yet habit was strong. She would turn to the Psalms, always a source of comfort and strength. She read 23 over twice, then 46, turning the words over and over. "God is our refuge and strength, a very present help in trouble." And she was in trouble, what kind she wasn't sure. All she knew was she had to ward off the sense of fear that threatened to overwhelm her.

Whatever happened, she had to remain with Allegra. No matter who wanted to frighten her away, she intended to stay.

Wearily she turned down the gas jet in her lamp but left it burning low. The light seemed to chase away the shadows that loomed in the corners.

Tired as she was, Nell could not sleep. She tossed restlessly. Her heart pounded, sounding loud in the night silence. But the house was not really silent. It seemed full of strange noises, haunting voices.

*N*ell tried to scream but couldn't; she tried to move but was unable. Panic-stricken, she tried to sit upright, struggling out of the twisted sheets. Finally, panting, perspiring, she sat up, pulling herself out of the nightmare. As she shivered in her damp nightgown, she realized that she had had a horrible dream. She took several deep breaths, trying to calm her thundering heart. It was then Nell became aware of noise— hushed voices, scurrying footsteps in the hall outside her bedroom.

She tossed aside the covers and got out of bed; hurrying barefoot to the door, she opened it.

The scene that met her eyes was one of confusion. Jewel, apron over her head, was weeping copiously. Mrs. Russell and Miss Benedict were arguing fiercely. Wallis, chalk faced, stood rigidly beside Jewel.

"What's going on?" Nell asked.

At the sound of Nell's voice, Jewel put her apron down, and she rushed to Nell's side, clutched her arm. "It's Tippy. Something's poisoned him."

"What?" Nell looked at Wallis, whose eyes were wide, red-rimmed. "How did it happen? He was fine last night."

Wallis bit her lower lip and explained in a husky voice, "I heard him whimpering sometime in the middle of the night. So as not to disturb Miss Allegra, I took him downstairs and put him outside. And he threw up. I thought mebbe it was something he got into while he was out with you in the afternoon." She eyed Nell accusingly. "Then I brought him back in and moved his basket into my room, so as not to waken Miss Allegra. I put him back in his basket, but this morning he was sick again." She shook her head. Nell could see Wallis's usual demeanor was shaken.

"Where is he now?" Nell asked.

"He's still in my room," Wallis replied.

"Come, I want to take a look at him," Nell said.

Murmuring as they went, Wallis led the way to her room, which was next to Allegra's.

"I dunno . . . if anything happens to this little dog, I don't know what Miss Allegra will do."

Tippy was lying halfway out of his basket, his mouth open. His white-coated tongue was lagging out of his mouth. Nell knelt down and put her hand on his head. His chin was resting on the edge of the basket, and he looked up at her with mournful dark eyes. She touched his nose, and it felt hot, dry. Allegra loved her dog; Nell knew they had to do something and do it fast.

"Sometimes animals cure themselves," said Jewel, who had followed them. "Mebbe he'll just sleep it off, whatever it is."

Nell nodded, not convinced. "Let's give him plenty of water; he may be thirsty. We'll just have to wait and see."

"What shall I tell Miss Allegra?" Wallis asked.

That was a problem. Tippy was supposed to sleep in his basket, but usually, at some point during the night, he managed to scuttle across the room, jump up on Allegra's bed,

167

snuggling into the eiderdown at the foot. If Tippy wasn't there when she awakened, Allegra would wonder.

Nell stood up, frowning. "Does Dr. Herbert come today?"

"Yes, miss, usually three mornings a week, sometimes more. Other days he calls in the afternoon and stays for dinner," Wallis answered.

"Perhaps we could get him to look at Tippy, suggest something to help. Until then, all we can do is hope and pray."

Nell was more concerned than she let on. If the adored little dog died, it could be a terrible blow for Allegra.

Miss Benedict was gone, but Mrs. Russell was still in the hall when Nell came back on her way to her bedroom.

"Bad, is it?" she asked Nell grimly.

"I'm afraid so. We're going to ask Dr. Herbert to examine Tippy when he comes; he may be able to suggest something to help."

"When you're dressed, Miss Winston, would you please come to my sitting room? I need to talk to you."

The housekeeper turned and went down the corridor, the keys on her belt jangling as she walked away.

Puzzled by the request, Nell hurried to her room, dressed, then went to Mrs. Russell's suite. Mrs. Russell invited her to sit down as if this were a social visit instead of a household crisis. On the table in front of the fireplace were a carafe, two cups, a plate of crumpets, and a pot of marmalade.

"I thought it would be cozier for us to have our morning coffee here and discuss privately our little problem. Miss Benedict's inclined to hysteria, and the maids, well—" she shrugged her plump shoulders, implying Nell knew what she meant.

"Cream and sugar?" Mrs. Russell's hand was poised to pour.

"Just black, please." Nell usually took cream, but after her dream-ridden night and this morning's dilemma, she needed a clear head and her wits about her.

She also refused the crumpets. Mrs. Russell spread hers

with a dollop of golden marmalade and took a bite. Nell sipped her coffee and waited.

"Well, now, Miss Winston, we have a bit of trouble on our hands. The situation needs to be dealt with as quickly and smoothly as possible. Poor Wallis is upset, but since she had no intention of causing such a calamity, she should not be blamed." Mrs. Russell smiled, adding significantly, "So no one should be the wiser, if you know what I mean."

Nell replaced her cup in its saucer, then put both down on the table in front of her. "No, Mrs. Russell, I don't think I do."

Mrs. Russell lowered her voice. "You see, my dear, Wallis has been with the Selkirks—the *other* Selkirks—since she went into service as a young girl; she became Mrs. Henrietta's lady's maid and has never had the slightest mark against her. That is why we must consider the whole thing a mistake. Not let it go any further. Especially to Miss Allegra. We wouldn't want this to cause Wallis's dismissal, now would we?"

"I don't understand. What has Wallis to do with Tippy's being ill?"

Mrs. Russell finished her coffee before answering.

"You know how she is about any kind of waste. Evidently Allegra didn't drink her milk last night; Wallis poured it into Tippy's bowl and he drank it. That's what made him sick. She had no idea—probably thought she was giving the little doggie a treat."

Nell stared at Mrs. Russell. What the housekeeper did not know was that she had not tasted her milk either. Had something in the milk made the little dog ill? Nell felt cold all over, as if she were standing in an icy rain. She heard Mrs. Russell's voice drone on, but she had slipped into another dimension. Had there been some kind of poison in the milk? Was it meant for Allegra or—or *her?* Nell tried but could not draw a full breath. She could just envision Wallis mumbling

"Waste not, want not" and giving the two cups of untouched milk to Tippy.

But Miss Benedict had been there too. She made no secret of the fact that she detested Allegra's pampered little pet. Had she done it maliciously? Or was Nell the original target? Had this been another scare tactic to drive her away from Hope's End, away from Allegra?

"So I'm sure you agree that we should keep this little mishap *entre nous.*"

Nell tried to snap herself back to the present. But something else gripped her: the needlepoint frame on which a large, rug-size canvas was stretched. To make such a piece, a heavyweight yarn would be needed. The background was a deep purple; Nell didn't remember for sure, but wasn't the yarn Jewel had brought her plum colored?

Suddenly Nell felt the urge to escape, to get away from Mrs. Russell's cloying persuasive voice. She didn't like the twist her thoughts had taken. Mrs. Russell had always been pleasant if distant to her. Nell had no reason to suspect the older woman might want to do her harm. But now everything seemed different, distorted. Nell had come to Hope's End with an optimistic spirit, but fear had become her constant companion.

That day Dr. Herbert did not come until late in the afternoon. He was advised immediately of Tippy's condition. Of course, Allegra had been told her pet was sick. She was beside herself with worry. When the doctor arrived, she insisted on being wheeled into Wallis's room while he examined the little dog. Both Nell and Jewel stood in the doorway beside her. Nell placed a hand on Allegra's shoulder and felt her trembling, and she was wringing her hands in anguish.

"He's evidently ingested something that could have been lethal," Dr. Herbert said. "Were you given a sedative last night, Allegra?"

She shook her head vehemently.

But the thought struck Nell, it *could* have been put there

without her permission. Lately, Allegra had protested when Miss Benedict suggested it. But it would be easy enough to slip it into her warm milk without her knowing. Maybe Tippy had gotten some. On occasion Nell had seen Allegra indulgently let the little dog sip from her cup of tea or glass of milk.

"I think the little fellow will survive. He got rid of most of it right away, I understand. Just give him plenty of fresh water and he'll probably be all right."

As much from relief as anything, Allegra burst into tears. She put her face in her hands, and her whole body was shaken with sobs.

"There, there, my dear." Dr. Herbert came to her side. "Your dog's going to recover. I'm almost sure of it. Now it's you we must take care of."

Nell still had her hand on Allegra's shoulder, and she felt the girl shudder. Allegra shrank back as Dr. Herbert approached.

He signaled to Jewel to turn the wheelchair around and push it back to Allegra's suite. As she did, Allegra grabbed Nell's hand, held it tight. Her mouth moved, forming the words, "Please, help me."

There was such pleading in them, such fear. Nell was stricken. She knew Dr. Herbert would not allow her to follow them. She also knew Allegra was terribly afraid, and she must find a way to help her.

*I*n her room, Nell paced the floor anxiously. Why was Allegra so terrified? Should she simply barge into Allegra's room and protect her? The word had come involuntarily. Did Allegra need to be protected from the very people who should offer her protection? So much was going on that was unexplainable.

Nell walked restlessly back and forth. At the bureau, she stopped, picked up the piece of yarn Jewel had found, and examined it. She shuddered. And did she also need protection? Had someone actually tried to harm her?

Was the yarn from Mrs. Russell's needlepoint? Miss Benedict's knitting? Wallis's workbasket? It always held an assortment. Wallis used odds and ends other people discarded to crochet multicolored mittens, mufflers, and caps for her innumerable nephews and nieces. What about Nanny's bag of scraps and twine? It was no use. Anyone could have taken the yarn from someone else's supply. That way it could not be traced. If only she would hear from Gervase Montgomery.

She must let Carrick know what had happened, what she suspected. Maybe his plan to get Allegra away was not as reckless as she had first thought. Out of harm's way was the phrase that came naturally. Distracted, she went to the window and looked out. It was already getting dark. The winter evenings came early. She peered out through the growing dusk, then stiffened. Leaning closer to the misty panes, she thought she saw something or someone moving in the garden. The figure of a man? Yes, she was sure it was. Maybe it was Carrick, anxious for word about Allegra. Maybe they had arranged a time to meet today, and he was waiting for her to come. He could have no idea what had happened that morning with Tippy. *Perhaps I should go out and tell him,* thought Nell.

Impulsively, Nell hurried out of her room and started down the stairs. As she reached the landing, she halted abruptly. Dr. Herbert and Miss Benedict were standing in the lower hall at the bottom of the staircase. Quickly she stepped back so as not to be seen. But she could hear them clearly.

"It was a stupid thing to do."

"But I thought you—"

"Don't try to assume you know what I want."

"I was only trying—"

"Don't. I can handle this in my own way."

What did Dr. Herbert mean? What had been a stupid thing for Miss Benedict to do?

Dr. Herbert's voice took on a steely edge. "It won't be long now. Desmond is arranging power of attorney. A matter of days at most."

"Then you will tell Mr. Selkirk I am to accompany Allegra to the clinic?"

"I never promised that, Clarise." Dr. Herbert seemed annoyed. "It has to look professional. One of the nursing sisters from my clinic will come, and it will be done in the most circumspect manner. No emotional partings, that sort of thing. For example, she cannot take the silly little dog."

"No, of course not." Miss Benedict gave a nervous little

laugh. "Surely you aren't placing me in the same category as her dog?"

"Don't be tiresome." Then he added, "You wouldn't be so easy to get rid of." He turned away. "Now, I have to speak to Desmond, make the final arrangements."

He started to walk away toward Mr. Selkirk's study, but Miss Benedict caught his arm, and his medical bag dropped. The catch must have come loose, and the contents spilled out onto the floor.

"Now look what you've done!" Dr. Herbert said angrily. He stooped to pick things up.

"Oh, Colin, I'm sorry." Rushing forward to help, she knelt down and began to gather the various items—tongue depressors, cotton swabs, small bottles.

"Don't!" he commanded harshly.

"I'm just trying to help."

"I don't need your help!"

"Why are you speaking to me like this?" she asked in a piteous voice. "After all I've done for you."

"I never asked you to do anything."

"But, I want to do what I can—"

Dr. Herbert was jamming things into his bag quickly and not in any kind of order. He stood up and glared at Clarise, who was still on her knees, looking up at him.

"Whatever you thought, I never promised you anything. Desmond and I had almost come to an agreement about Allegra until this happened. Now just stay out of it." With this, he turned on his heels and walked over to the closed door of Mr. Selkirk's study. After a staccato rap, he opened the door and went in, shutting it behind him.

Clarise sat back on her heels and buried her face in her hands. Nell was outraged. No matter that Miss Benedict had openly displayed dislike of her, Nell hated to see anyone humiliated. Dr. Herbert had shown himself to be the heartless person Nell had suspected from the beginning.

Descending the stairs slowly, Nell wondered whether she

should offer sympathy or pretend she hadn't witnessed the scene. Before she could speak, Clarise turned, looked over her shoulder, and saw Nell. She scrambled to her feet. However, one heel caught in the hem of her skirt, and she staggered. Nell ran down the rest of the steps. "Here, let me help you."

Clarise jerked away, her face mottled, her mouth twisted. "No, don't touch me. I don't want your help." She spoke angrily. "I don't need anyone's help."

She brushed by Nell and hurried up the stairway. Nell stood looking after her for a minute. Then remembering why she had come down in the first place, she went down the hall, through the conservatory, and into the cloakroom. She grabbed the ulster and went out into the dark garden.

There was no one in sight. Could she have been mistaken? Nell walked all the way down the path that led to the lake. She couldn't see anything. If that had been Carrick, he would have made himself visible by now. Perhaps he had grown tired of waiting and left. She would have to contact him some other way. The wind off the lake was cold. Nell pulled the ulster closely around her and went back into the house.

Desmond's study door was still shut, but Nell could hear the male voices from behind it. They were loud enough to be heard but not understood. She felt reasonably sure Dr. Herbert and Desmond Selkirk were having a heated discussion.

Nell started to go up the steps when the toe of her shoe hit something and sent it rolling on the polished floor. Nell saw it was a small bottle. It must have fallen out of Dr. Herbert's medical bag. Quickly, she picked it up and looked at it. It held a gray liquid she recognized as the same the doctor poured out and gave Allegra the night of the Christmas ball. The stuff that made her sleep so heavily.

A chill prickled down Nell's neck along her spine. She had thought the sedative too strong then and she still thought so. Had he administered it again today? It would seem unwarranted if he had. Certainly Allegra's reaction to her beloved pet's near poisoning was natural, not the hysterical kind she had had after Carrick's sudden appearance at the Christmas ball and the scene with her uncle that followed.

Nell's heart pounded. She hoped that had not happened. Pocketing the bottle, she went up the stairs. Determined to see for herself, she marched right to Allegra's suite.

She was met by Wallis, who put a warning forefinger up to her mouth, then whispered that Allegra was sound asleep and would probably sleep for hours. So, Dr. Herbert *had* administered the same sedative after all. Nell felt angry at herself for not accompanying Allegra back to her room earlier. Perhaps she could have prevented this. However, probably not. Dr. Herbert seemed to be in a position to do whatever he wanted at Hope's End.

After a troubled night, Nell got up the following morning with a plan firmly in mind. She would walk to the village, go to a chemist shop, and find out what kind of sedative was in the bottle from Dr. Herbert's bag. She hoped he hadn't missed it.

After breakfast, Nell checked on Allegra. Wallis said she had slept through the night and was still asleep.

"When she wakes up, be sure to tell her I want to see her." Wallis nodded and started to close the door, but Nell put out her hand to check her. "Wallis, whether you believe it or not, I love Miss Allegra. I have her best interests at heart. I wish you wouldn't resent me."

Wallis looked startled at such frankness. But Nell felt it was important that the maid, as devoted as she was to her mistress, understood that.

The other thing Nell decided was to take Jewel into her confidence, at least to a degree. She did not want the maid to be too involved so as to endanger her job. But knowing her loyalty was with Allegra, she would be useful if Nell needed her help. So before Jewel left for the day, Nell gave her a note to deliver to Carrick asking him to meet her at the tearoom in the village. He ought to know the threat to Allegra was closer than they had imagined.

Before leaving, Nell checked again on Allegra. She discovered Allegra had awakened but was still drowsy. Tippy, limp but apparently recovered, was curled up beside her in the bed. Nell went over to the bed; leaning close to Allegra's ear, she whispered, "I'll be back later."

Allegra's eyelids fluttered, and she attempted a smile. Nell squeezed her hand, patted Tippy, and left.

It was a raw, cold day. The wind whipped Nell's skirt, tore at her bonnet strings, and penetrated her coat. Heavy dark clouds roiled above a gray sky, threatening rain. But Nell, too preoccupied with her errand, had not thought to bring an umbrella.

As she was hurrying down the street, she saw Hamilton Lewis going in the entrance of The Red Fox Inn. Quickly she stepped back into a doorway, not wanting to be seen. Much as she enjoyed his company and was flattered by his attention, her errand was desperate and much too important to be diverted.

As soon as he had disappeared into the restaurant, she dashed back out again. She walked down main street to the small apothecary shop tucked between two buildings with jutting roofs.

She pushed the door open, and the wind caught it and slammed it back against the wall. The noise rattled the bottles on the shelves and brought a startled looking man in a cotton apron out from a room behind the counter. He had on spectacles, and his gray hair stood out around his head like a dandelion.

"Good gracious!" he exclaimed, regarding her over his glasses that had slid slightly down his long, thin nose. "Sounds like there's quite a storm blowing up out there. What can I do for you, young lady? Cold medicine or a cough syrup? This time of year is the worst for all sorts of ailments."

"No, thank you; I'm in good health, thank heavens," Nell

replied. "I just wanted to find out what is in this bottle. A friend of mine has taken it, and I would like to know what it is." She dug into her reticule, pulled out the small vial, and handed it to him.

The man took it and held it up to the light, examining it with narrowed eyes; then he removed the cap and sniffed. His mouth pursed thoughtfully as he looked over at Nell, regarding her for a few seconds before saying, "Why, bless my soul, miss; I hope your friend has not taken too much of this."

"Why? What is it? Could it harm her?"

"This is chloral, miss. A very potent drug, highly addictive."

Dazed and sick at heart, Nell left the chemist shop. The air had become even colder; the wind was piercing as she started walking. Deep in her disturbing thoughts, she didn't realize until she had gone clear to the end of the lane that she was going in the wrong direction. A little disoriented, she turned and crossed the street and began walking up the other way.

What the chemist had told her had frightened her badly. If Dr. Herbert had been giving Allegra chloral regularly for all her minor upsets, it was reckless. He must know the possible dangers of overuse the chemist had emphasized. Or should have. Was he ignoring them, or did he just not care?

Dr. Herbert was ready to carry out his plan to take Allegra to his clinic, and Desmond had probably convinced Allegra to sign papers giving him control of the estate. Things were moving fast; Allegra was in danger. But of a different kind than Nell had suspected after the poisoning of the milk. That had been meant for *her,* just as the planned fall on the stairway. Did someone feel the best way to accomplish all this was to remove Nell from the scene? By whatever means? Nell shuddered. She needed help. But from whom?

If only there were someone wiser, older she could confide in about all this. Oh, why had Gervase gone away? Who else could she possibly tell her awful suspicions to? The thought of Hamilton Lewis came to mind. Did she dare? He was certainly sensitive, genuinely concerned about Allegra, trustworthy. It would be going beyond the rigid code of their acquaintance. However, the situation was serious enough to break the social rules.

Deep in thought, Nell started walking up the street when something halted her abruptly. Desmond Selkirk was emerging from the entrance of The Red Fox Inn accompanied by Hamilton Lewis. They were soon joined by Dr. Herbert. What did Hamilton have to do with these two?

A horrible explanation thrust itself unwanted into Nell's mind. Was Hamilton "the clever lawyer" Desmond had told his wife he was going to employ to break Gervase's guardianship, to obtain power to control Allegra's fortune, her fate? Nell ducked into a nearby doorway to avoid being seen. A few minutes later she saw the three men part; Dr. Herbert and Desmond walked together toward The White Knight pub, and Hamilton walked to his horse hitched to a post outside The Red Fox Inn.

Had the trio met to insure that all was done legally yet deviously, while Gervase was out of the country and Allegra was helpless? Nell drew a deep breath. How could Hamilton be a party to such a nefarious undertaking?

Nell was sick with disappointment at the idea that the man she admired had turned traitor. How could she, Carrick, and Allegra defeat such formidable foes? Two strong-willed, power-hungry men backed by a clever lawyer. Did they have a chance to unmask such villains and their accomplices?

Nell had suspected someone else was aiding them, someone on the outside. Now she was sure and shocked at the probability of who it was.

She waited a few minutes longer, then started back up the street. To her utter dismay, just as she reached the corner, Hamilton Lewis was coming toward her. There was no way to escape. They were face-to-face. His serious expression turned to one of genuine pleasure. But it chilled her. How could he be such a hypocrite? He had seemed so compassionate about Allegra, how could he aid and abet those who would so mistreat her?

"Miss Winston." Hamilton greeted her. "What a happy coincidence."

"Good day, Mr. Lewis," she replied coolly and started to move to pass him with a chilly nod.

His face lost its bright pleasure. "Wait, please, Miss Winston, may I not entice you to have a cup of tea with me at the Buttercup?"

"No, thank you, Mr. Lewis. I am on my way there now to meet a *friend*."

He looked amused. "And am I not a friend as well, Miss Winston?" he asked playfully.

Nell drew herself up haughtily. "That is a matter of opinion. Good day," Nell said and kept walking up the street.

Hamilton caught up with her. "Please, have I done something to offend you, Miss Winston? If so, I declare it was unintentional and wish sincerely to apologize for whatever it was."

She halted and said icily, "That is for you to decide, Mr. Lewis. Now, I must be on my way."

Her meeting with Carrick was brief but charged with emotion. When Nell told him about the chloral, his face flushed angrily and he banged a clenched fist on the table. Several people turned to look at their table, and Nell leaned closer. "Please. We must keep our wits about us. Everything must be done in good order and planned carefully so that we will not be outsmarted." Quickly they went over their plan.

When they came out of the tearoom, it was growing dark. Nell had a long way to go, and since Carrick had come on horseback, she would have to go alone.

Nell had only covered a short distance when once again she began to have the distinct feeling she was being followed. She spun around. If someone were stalking her, she would confront him. Clenching her hands, she stood there a minute but saw nothing. She told herself it was just her imagination. In spite of that, she walked faster. She couldn't let herself become a nervous wreck. If she were going to help Allegra, she would have to keep her mind steady, her wits about her.

At last she saw the gates and the jagged rooftop of the house beyond and felt an irrational sense of relief. Soon she would be safe inside the four walls of the house. Although, if the truth were told, the Selkirk house had not proved a safe place for her.

The darkness was impenetrable now, and Nell pushed through the gates and hurried up the driveway. She would take a shortcut through the garden then enter the house through the cloakroom.

She had just reached the center of the garden when someone suddenly grabbed her from behind and thrust her against the brick edge of the fishpond. A strong arm went around her right shoulder, pressing against her throat; the other hand gripped the back of her neck, forcing down her head and her upper body until she was bent double.

She tried to scream, cry out, but only a strangled sound came forth before her head was thrust into the cold water and held there. Water flowed into her eyes and nose. Her brain flashed her a warning not to open her mouth or water could rush in, flooding her lungs. The awful realization that she was being drowned made her feel desperate, helpless.

She never knew how long those iron hands held her under the water, but suddenly they let go, and she lifted her head, gasping and choking. Her bonnet had fallen off, her hair was dripping, the front of her coat was soaked. Wrenching herself away from those punishing hands, she put one hand out to steady herself on the slippery brick rim of the fishpond. With the back of her arm she wiped her eyes, trying to see her attacker through the murky dark. But all she saw was a fleeing figure soon lost to sight in the dark garden.

Shaking, frightened, her aching lungs struggling for breath, Nell stared into the threatening darkness. In spite of her wet clothes, perspiration flowed over her, the cold sweat of terror. Someone had tried to kill her.

Her knees suddenly weak, Nell leaned against the fishpond. She looked up and saw the thin sliver of the moon sliding through the clouds. It looked so peaceful, so benign. She murmured, "It is so beautiful. I was afraid I'd never see it again. Thank you, God."

She shivered and knew she had to get inside, out of her wet things. Who had been her attacker? Had someone followed her? Or waited for her here? Who had tried to kill her? It would have been easy enough to keep her submerged until she lost consciousness. Why had the attacker released her? Had this been just another warning from someone who desperately wanted her to leave Hope's End?

25

*I*n her room, Nell quickly rid herself of her wet clothes. Only then did she realize her reticule containing the chloral bottle was missing. She must have dropped it during the attack. That realization brought another: Without it she had no evidence.

Evidence of what, she wasn't sure. To confront Dr. Herbert on the dangerous treatment he was giving Allegra? To inform the Selkirks? Or Gervase?

Much as she dreaded it, she knew she must go back to the garden and look for it. Returning to the scene of the brutal attack horrified her. But there was no alternative. She had to go.

As she stood there momentarily dazed and hesitant, a tap came on the door and Jewel entered. She looked curiously at the wet clothes discarded on the floor and cast a questioning glance at Nell as she bent to pick them up.

"Cook wanted to know if it would suit you to have supper on a tray. Miss Benedict is having hers in her room. Says she's not feeling well."

No wonder, Nell thought, *after that scene with Dr. Herbert.*

"Yes, that will be fine, Jewel; if it's not too much trouble," Nell replied.

"No trouble at all, miss," Jewel said. "Would you want me to take these things down to the drying room?" That innocent question begged further explanation, and Jewel waited for an answer.

Nell decided not to tell the girl about the attack in the garden. At least not until she had had more time to think about it herself. So she just said, "Thank you, Jewel, if you would."

Jewel left, and Nell got a towel and brush and started drying her hair. There was no use denying it. Someone had malevolent intentions toward her. She was in as much jeopardy as Allegra. The so-called accidents had not been accidents at all but were designed with one purpose—to get rid of Nell one way or another. And Allegra. What was to be her fate if Nell were gone? Unable to get in touch with Gervase, it was up to Nell to protect her. The only right thing to do was to tell Allegra everything.

Nell was still shaky from her ordeal, but while everyone was in the dining room, she slipped downstairs and forced herself back to the fishpond. A pale moon, escaped from the earlier clouds, lent a mysterious light. However, it did not shed enough for Nell to see. She got down on her hands and knees, searching with as wide a pattern as she could in the grass at the base of the brick wall. She could find nothing. Beginning to shiver, she finally decided she would have to wait until the first light of morning and come back then.

Instinctively, Nell felt Allegra was a great deal stronger than anyone else thought. She must know the truth about the plots against her. Nell repeated to herself what she strongly believed: "Ye shall know the truth, and the truth shall make you free."

Nell waited for the house to quiet down so she could slip into Allegra's room. She kept repeating John 8:32 to herself as she crept down the hall to Allegra's suite. Filled with trepidation, she quietly turned the knob of Allegra's door, never imagining that it would be she herself who was in for a greater shock.

When Nell entered Allegra's bedroom, she saw that Allegra was holding a book in her hands, although she did not seem to be reading. Stepping into the soft light shed by the lamp beside Allegra's bed, Nell said quietly, "Allegra, I didn't mean to startle you, but I need to talk to you."

Allegra smiled, put her book aside, and motioned Nell closer. Nell moved to the side of the bed, sat down, and took Allegra's hand in both of her own.

"What I have to tell you may frighten you, but I believe you are strong enough to hear it."

Allegra's eyes widened curiously; she looked puzzled.

"Do you trust me, Allegra?" Nell asked.

Allegra nodded emphatically.

"Good. You can also trust Carrick and your uncle Gervase. You know your uncle does not believe your paralysis is permanent. He believes the shock you suffered in the accident has somehow paralyzed you, but you can recover and walk again. Something is blocking that. Can you think back and remember exactly what happened that might have caused this?"

Allegra did not seem surprised but nodded. She turned very pale, however, and drew a long shuddering sigh. Then to Nell's amazement, Allegra said, "Nell, I have something to tell you too."

Nell gasped, "You can talk! When did your voice come back?"

"Some time ago, but I was afraid—"

As if startled by the sound of Allegra's voice, Tippy raised his head from the depths of the quilt, looked from one to the other, then curled up again and went back to sleep.

"What were you afraid of, Allegra? Or whom?" Nell asked. Haltingly the story began to pour out. Allegra and her parents were on their way to a New Year's Day party at one of their friend's homes in the country. There had been snow, and the roads were icy; then had come a sudden thaw, making them muddy, slick, and treacherous. Allegra did not know exactly what had caused the accident; one of the horses had slipped, and the others had been dragged down with him, toppling the carriage. All she knew was that it had turned sideways, the doors had flown open, and she was thrown free.

"I must have hit my head, and I was knocked unconscious," Allegra said. "All I remember is opening my eyes and seeing the sky and wondering what I was doing lying in a field. I tried to move, but something pinned me down; part of the axle with a wheel attached had fallen on my legs. It hurt but not badly. However, I was dazed. Then I saw him."

"Whom did you see, Allegra?"

Allegra shivered, and Nell put her arms around her and held her tight for a few minutes. Slowly Allegra went on.

"Dr. Herbert. I recalled that he'd been at the crossroads on horseback earlier. We'd passed him on our way, and we all waved to him. He was—a friend of the family." Allegra's mouth trembled. "I don't know how long it was before he came along. It seemed ages that I was there alone. I had raised myself on my elbows and could see Mama. She was lying close by, maybe a yard or two away, but quite still. And then I saw my father sprawled on the ground some distance away. I wanted to go to them, but I couldn't. My father's head was bleeding. I saw all this blood, and I was so afraid. He was moaning as if in terrible pain." Allegra caught her breath.

"Then I saw Dr. Herbert. He came riding up on his horse, and when he saw the accident, he dismounted. He looked at my father very briefly then rushed over to where my mother was lying. I think she may have already been dead. She had lain there so long without moving, without making a sound." Allegra stopped again as if it was a supreme effort for her to go on.

"The look on Dr. Herbert's face was—was ghastly. He knelt

down beside my mother, and I could hear him saying her name. Over and over. 'Henrietta, beloved.' I guess that shocked me as much as anything. Him calling her beloved." Allegra shook her head slightly.

"He took her hand, pressed it to his mouth, and began to weep. Uncontrollably. The most awful sounds. I'd never heard a man crying before, and it was devastating. I knew then Mama must be dead." Allegra put her fists up to her mouth, her eyes fixed as if she were reliving the scene. "He just stayed there, bent over her, moaning. He didn't even look over at my father. Even when he called." Allegra swallowed hard.

"I heard Father call, 'Please, someone, help me.' I struggled to get up, but the carriage wheel was on top of me. My father needed me desperately, and I couldn't go to him. But worse still, Dr. Herbert, who *could* have really helped him, didn't. He was holding my mother, cradling her in his arms like you'd hold a child. I heard my father call again. This time his voice was weaker. And still Dr. Herbert didn't go, and finally, my father didn't call anymore." Allegra's eyes brimmed with tears.

"Can you believe it? A doctor! And a man is in terrible pain and he ignores him? I started to scream, 'Dr. Herbert, help my father! For mercy's sake, please help him!' I was calling as loud as I could. So loud I could feel the muscles in my throat straining. Still he didn't move. He gave me one hate-filled glance as if he detested me for being alive when my mother was dead. He lay my mother down very gently on the ground, took off his cape, and covered her with it. Then he pulled off his scarf, rolled it up, and fitted it into a pillow under her head. Very deliberately he got up and walked to the end of the road. There he stood, head bowed, until the rescuers arrived." Allegra gulped for breath. She had been relaying this story so fast she was breathless.

"By that time, my father wasn't making any sound at all. I was crying and was hoarse from yelling. When the rescuers came, they righted the carriage. They brought stretchers and talked among themselves. One man came over to where I was and spoke very kindly to me; he said they would work fast to lift the wheel off me. But I kept protesting, 'My father is badly hurt; go to him first.' The man just shook his head and said sympathetically, 'Sorry, miss; the gentleman's past help. He's dead.' Shock must have set in then. Maybe I fainted. I don't know.

"The next thing I remember is Dr. Herbert bending over me. His eyes were like knives boring into me. I hated him, and I screamed, 'You murderer! You let my father bleed to death!' The other man looked at him, but Dr. Herbert remained icy calm. He shoved the man aside and said, 'The girl's hysterical.' Then he leaned over me, very close, put his face right up to mine, and said between clenched teeth, 'Shut up, you little fool.' Even though I was terrified, I screamed back at him, 'You let my father die!' He slapped me as hard as he could. It almost snapped my neck it was so hard. It shocked me silent all right. He put his head down to my ear and whispered, 'If you ever say that again, I'll kill you.'

"Everything went black after that. I must have lost consciousness. The next thing I knew, I was here in my own bed. Wallis, Jewel, and Nanny, all looking scared, were gathered around it. And then I saw him—Dr. Herbert—standing at the foot of my bed. He was glaring at me. I shrank back, wondering if he was really going to kill me in front of all these people. I knew he wouldn't do that. But that look he gave me, I knew he had meant what he said at the scene of the accident. I opened my mouth to say something, and that's when I found I couldn't speak. I'd lost my voice. Somehow it had registered in my brain that if I ever spoke—no matter what I said—I'd be killed."

Nell was appalled but not surprised at Dr. Herbert's villainy. She had never liked nor trusted him. She had sensed a darkness in him. Now her reasons were confirmed.

"He has convinced my uncle Desmond that I should go

to his private clinic to be cared for," Allegra continued. "He tells him I'll recover better there under his supervision. But what he means is under his control."

"But the other doctors your uncle consulted, did they not agree it might be from shock?"

Allegra shrugged. "Dr. Herbert just *said* he had consulted with specialists. He told Uncle Desmond that I might never regain my speech."

"It was to his advantage that you didn't," mused Nell.

"Yes, Uncle Gervase held the view that my losing my voice and being unable to move my legs were both results of shock. Of course, he didn't know the real reason."

"And Dr. Herbert wasn't going to take the chance that anyone found out different." Nell was thoughtful. "Does Carrick know any of this?"

"Not all of it." Allegra's eyes brightened. "He does know I can speak. It started coming back gradually. I tested it when I was alone. But I was still afraid to let Dr. Herbert know. I didn't know what to do. Until you came, Nell. Thank God you came." Allegra squeezed Nell's hand. "When you arranged for Carrick and me to meet, I felt there was some hope. So I told him. He wants to wait until Uncle Gervase comes back from the continent and ask if we can become engaged. Then I can get free of Dr. Herbert." For a brief moment Allegra looked happy.

"And your legs. The paralysis must be as Gervase suspected—also the result of trauma."

"I've thought about that too. The wheel and axle were heavy; I was bruised but not seriously injured by them. I have come to my own conclusion. The fact that I wanted desperately to go to my father but was trapped and couldn't may also be the emotional shock." A faint smile touched her lips. "I may walk again."

"I'm sure you will if we can just—"

Allegra's expression changed, and her eyes darkened. "Yes, we must think of what to do. Dr. Herbert has persuaded

Uncle Desmond to move me to his clinic near London. They would have to get Uncle Gervase's permission unless . . . I heard them discussing the possibility of Uncle Desmond getting power of attorney to handle everything. That's what I'm afraid of. If Uncle Gervase doesn't return soon, they might just do it."

"Allegra, you will have to confront Dr. Herbert before witnesses. You may have to go before a magistrate and swear that he neglected his professional duty in not going to the aid of your father. Doctors take an oath that they will do whatever they can to save lives. We must get help."

Nell was beginning to realize what a big problem they had and how few resources. They were but two young women with little or no experience of the world against two men—one with diabolic intent, the other greedy, power hungry, and facing financial ruin, unless he could get hold of his wealthy niece's funds.

"Yes, we must have a plan," Allegra agreed calmly.

Nell was gratified; her belief in Allegra's inner strength had been validated. In spite of her fragility, Allegra was a person of strong character, who wanted justice not only for herself but for her wronged parent.

They talked until almost dawn; both were exhausted and emotionally spent. Before Nell left, they agreed to keep secret Allegra's restored voice. In the meantime, Carrick may have reached Gervase. Even now Allegra's uncle might be on his way back to England. They needed him—his support and possibly his protection. Exposing Dr. Herbert would be dangerous.

26

*N*ell walked swiftly back down the hall and into her bedroom. She closed the door and leaned against it wearily. Her emotions were strained almost to the breaking point. She knew it must be even more so for Allegra. All the anger, all the fear that had been suppressed so long, locked within Allegra, had to come out. She was stronger now, Nell felt, ready to face whatever had to be faced.

Nell trembled thinking of the hazardous road ahead of them. Time was of the essence. Dr. Herbert must live in daily fear that Allegra would recover her speech and thus have the courage to accuse him of his crimes. His aim must have been to keep Allegra sufficiently sedated with chloral so that she was helpless to resist his recommendation that she go to his clinic. Evidently he had convinced Desmond that only thus could he get control of his niece's estate and get himself out of debt. It was a despicable plot, and Nell was determined to thwart them. However, the combined forces of Desmond Selkirk and Colin Herbert now enforced by legal aid from Hamilton Lewis seemed formidable.

Again Nell felt the pain of disillusionment. She had always

prided herself on being a good judge of character. In Hamilton Lewis she had been completely deluded.

"Wisdom is what I need, Lord," Nell murmured sleepily, as she finally crawled into bed and pulled the quilt over her shoulders.

She was just about to drift off when she remembered with a start that she had to go back into the garden to look for her reticule. With a heavy sigh, she dragged herself up again and made her way along the hallway, down the stairs, through the silent house out to the garden.

With the eerie light of dawn, Nell crept downstairs and outside to the garden. She ran over the dew-soaked grass to the fishpond. Last night's attack was still vivid, and she had a hard time keeping her teeth from chattering. In the shredded wisps of early morning mist swirling about her, Nell saw her reticule at the base of the fishpond. Picking it up, she checked inside. The half-filled bottle of chloral was in it. Whoever had attacked her had not known about it or was not interested in anything but frightening her badly. On the label was some sort of medical symbol that could probably be traced to Dr. Herbert. Nell had her evidence if and when she needed it.

That afternoon, Nell set out with Tippy, ostensibly on her daily outing with the little dog. Everything had to look normal. Nothing suspect. Nell and Allegra were restricted in their communication. Both were afraid they might somehow slip and reveal Allegra's ability to speak.

Going over and over in her mind their midnight discussion and the strategy Carrick was working out so preoccupied Nell that she did not realize she had come as far as the village. She decided to go to the tearoom for some refreshment before starting her walk back. It was then she was startled to see Hamilton Lewis dismounting in front of The Red Fox Inn. Nell felt the wrench of her disappointment in him. Was he meeting again with his partners, Desmond Selkirk and Dr. Herbert? She decided to watch to see if the other two joined him.

She scooped up Tippy and tucked him under her cape and went into the tearoom. Luckily, a table by the window was empty, offering a good vantage point from which to observe the entrance of The Red Fox Inn.

Keeping Tippy concealed, she gave her order to the unsuspecting waitress. When it came, Nell made a pretense of drinking her tea while she maintained a lookout on the street. So as not to be noticed by the proprietress, who might take a dim view of animals in her spotless tearoom, Nell held Tippy on her lap and fed him tidbits of her scone to keep him quiet. She lingered while her tea grew cold and Tippy became restless, but there was no sign of Dr. Herbert or Desmond Selkirk. Well, even though the odds were against them, Nell was determined she, Carrick, and Allegra would outsmart them.

The next two days were fraught with anxiety. Nell felt at any moment Dr. Herbert might exercise his plan. She tried to discern any difference in Desmond's behavior, in his routine, or demeanor at the dinner table. Was he less tense, less gruff now that he had found a way out of his financial crisis?

Fortunately, the early March weather turned mild with a false spring. So Allegra's outing in the garden could be arranged with little problem. Nell had told Jewel as much as she needed to know. The maid, an avid reader of penny romance books, accepted the idea that Allegra and Carrick were going to elope to frustrate her uncle Desmond.

"Them two was meant for each other," she said with an emphatic nod. It was easy enough for her to pack a few things of Allegra's and hide them in the baskets of laundry she carried up and down the stairs daily. She would secrete them somewhere until Nell gave further word on where to bring them. Tickled at the idea of being in on a wildly romantic escapade, Jewel was as good as her word.

For the next few days, they would follow the routine they had established. Nell would wheel Allegra along the winding paths, always ending up at the far end of the garden, where Carrick would meet her.

At this point, Nell, sure she could be seen by anyone who was watching, would walk back to the house as if she had left Allegra alone, sunning, reading, or simply enjoying the view of the lake and the early sunset. Actually, Allegra would either be sitting in Carrick's boat or practicing walking.

With every day that passed, Nell prayed that Gervase would return. There was so much risk for everyone if they carried out this plan. Especially when they had no real evidence against Dr. Herbert or Desmond. It was only to be followed through if the doctor openly announced with Desmond's approval that Allegra was to go to his clinic.

While searching hopefully for a letter from Gervase, Nell found a note from Hamilton Lewis one day in the morning post. It was short and to the point.

> My dear Miss Winston, Please meet me at The Red Fox Inn Thursday morning at ten o'clock. I urge you to put aside any personal animosity and comply with this request. It is a matter of utmost importance.
> With kind regards, your servant,
> Hamilton Lewis

Nell debated. Was he trying to get her to help them persuade Allegra to go to Dr. Herbert's clinic, sign the power of attorney over to her uncle? Her first impulse was to simply tear up the note, ignore it. Then her curiosity overcame her suspicion. She had no real proof of Hamilton's involvement in this matter except her own sight of him with people she despised. Perhaps it would be helpful to meet him. Perhaps it was worth finding out if what she suspected was true.

Thursday morning, Nell mentioned casually she was going to the village on some errands. On her way, she found herself rehearsing what she might say to Hamilton if he did admit to representing Desmond Selkirk. Was he simply helping his younger brother's cause in his courtship of Felicity? Such motives did not match the man she had thought so highly of—at least until now. Wait and see, Nell told herself.

At The Red Fox Inn, she went in the ladies' entrance, circumventing the tavern, and up to the reception desk. The clerk eyed her skeptically. "I am to meet a Mr. Hamilton Lewis here," Nell said in her haughtiest voice.

The clerk glanced at her, taking in the stylish bonnet, the well-cut walking suit of glen plaid trimmed with braid. He raised an eyebrow. "You were to meet this gentleman where, miss?"

Annoyed, Nell glanced around. Why hadn't Hamilton been waiting for her instead of putting her through this embarrassing interrogation? At just that moment she heard his deep voice, "Miss Winston, thank you for coming." To the clerk he said authoritatively, "We will be in my private quarters upstairs."

He held out his arm to Nell, who drew back slightly. *Private quarters?* What did that mean?

"Don't be alarmed, Miss Winston," Hamilton said in a low voice. "Someone is very anxious to see you and speak to you. Trust me, please."

They went up a short flight of stairs, down a hall to a closed door at one end. Hamilton knocked once and opened the door, allowing Nell to precede him into the room.

A man was standing at the fireplace, his back to the door. When he turned, Nell gasped, "Mr. Montgomery!"

"Sorry to startle you, my dear. I don't enjoy playing this kind of cloak-and-dagger game. But as we shall soon inform you, it has been necessary."

Nell was glad when Hamilton drew up a chair to the hearth for her because her knees felt suddenly weak.

"Oh, Mr. Montgomery, if you only knew how much I've longed to see you, talk to you, tell you—" she began.

"I can only imagine, my dear." Gervase nodded, regarding her kindly. "And before anything else, I want you to know how impressed I am with your loyalty and support of my dear niece." He paused. "There is much to tell you. And I want you to know my silence and absence have not been indifference to what has been going on at Hope's End; however, it was necessary to what I was trying to do. I will take things one at a time. But first, I want to commend Hamilton here for his skillful handling of the situation while I have been out of the country."

Nell glanced at Hamilton. Ashamed of her resentment toward him, her face grew warm. She busied herself pulling off her kid gloves; then she clasped her hands in her lap and leaned forward to listen attentively to what Gervase was saying.

"As you no doubt are aware, Colin Herbert has convinced Desmond that Allegra's recovery would be assured if she were to go to his private clinic and be placed under his exclusive care. He has long been trying to persuade Allegra to agree."

"Yes, I know. But she doesn't—" Nell wondered if Gervase had any idea why Allegra kept refusing—that she was deathly afraid of Dr. Herbert.

"True. *He* contends it is because she has too many people surrounding her who keep her wrapped in cotton wool with no chance to recover—anticipating her needs and so forth." Gervase looked thoughtful. "Of course, he may have a point. But that is not his real reason for wanting Desmond to have the power to override her objections, *for her own good,* you understand." These words were sarcastically emphasized. "However, as you know, I was desperate to find any cure that might bring Allegra back to her normal healthy state. So I decided to investigate." He halted, and his expression became very grim.

"What I discovered was that this clinic of Dr. Herbert's is not in the countryside south of London as he has inferred but in Switzerland. Oh, he has a few patients, mostly hysterical rich women, who want a few weeks' rest at his country estate . . . but it is not a clinic. The clinic he has in mind for Allegra is in a small Swiss village, picturesque, but very remote; six months of the year it is virtually cut off from the outside world by deep snow. When I found this out, I decided to investigate further. That's where I've been, my dear. In Switzerland. The clinic is a chalet owned by Dr. Herbert, and the staff consists of a couple, a very nice couple, who speak no English. It is there Dr. Herbert plans to take Allegra."

Nell gasped. "But I don't understand—"

"He was very much in love with my sister, Henrietta, Allegra's mother, whom she resembles very much. In some distorted way, Dr. Herbert thinks he can have his lost love back in the person of Allegra. Oh, he may very well think he can restore her to health. Switzerland is a beautiful, healthful place; everyone knows that. But it is a monstrous idea to take a young woman against her will and try to control her life."

"But she is afraid of him!" Nell burst out. Then realizing neither Gervase nor Hamilton knew the real story of what happened at the scene of the fatal accident, she clapped one hand over her mouth. Should she tell them? Would that be violating Allegra's confidence? Putting her in more danger?

Both men looked at her curiously. Then Gervase went on. "Colin is a very assertive fellow, used to getting his own way, lording it over others. Desmond is putty in his hands. He would agree to anything the doctor proposed. This would enable him to take over the management of Allegra's affairs. But as long as I am Allegra's guardian they cannot do anything. They have tried. That's where Hamilton has been of the greatest help. He found out through a fellow barrister that Desmond was petitioning the courts to have my guardianship contested on the basis I was out of the country and neglecting my duties on Allegra's behalf. He was asking to be temporarily appointed guardian in my place until I returned to England and gave valid reasons why I had not been attending my niece. That would be almost impossible to prove. However, given the right lawyer, it could be slipped through." He glanced at Hamilton approvingly and said, "Hamilton, who is *my* attorney, knew where to locate me and apprise me of what was going on."

Gervase paused again. "I have been back for some weeks now, staying here at the Red Fox incognito, watching the house, the comings and goings and—" an ironic smile touched his mouth "—and trying to keep my eye on you. I didn't want anything to happen to you, my dear. And you did make yourself pretty vulnerable to anyone with malice on their mind."

Nell's eyes grew large. "Have you been in the garden? Did you follow me from the village?"

Gervase nodded solemnly. "Yes, I'm afraid so. Did I frighten you?"

"Half out of my mind," Nell declared. "But it certainly wasn't you that night by the fishpond?"

"The fishpond?" Gervase frowned.

Quickly Nell described the attack. Both men looked angry.

"I wouldn't put it past Colin to hire someone for a few shillings and a pint or two," Gervase said.

Nell decided she must tell them all she knew about the chloral and the real danger she felt Allegra was in. She assured them that Carrick was working with all his heart to help Allegra, and the young couple wanted to marry.

"We must get Allegra away from Hope's End." Gervase stood up and began to pace the room. "Before anything drastic happens."

Quickly she told them what she and Carrick had resolved to do if the worst happened. Suddenly aware of how much time had passed, Nell consulted her pendant watch. "I must get back."

"I'll take you," Hamilton said at once. "I have my small buggy; it will be much faster than walking."

Promising to be in touch with her as soon as he had decided exactly how to take charge of the legal matters and confront Desmond, Gervase thanked Nell again and she left with Hamilton.

Hamilton helped Nell carefully into the trap and climbed into the driver's seat; he tapped his whip lightly on the horse's flanks, and they were off. As they approached Hope's End, Nell directed him around to the wagon entrance near the stable. "It would be better if I were not seen with you," she said.

When Hamilton reined his horse, Nell started to get out, but he put a restraining hand on her arm. "Wait, please, Miss Winston. Are we friends again?"

"Oh yes, Mr. Lewis, and I am sorry I ever thought—"

"You had every reason to wonder. I sincerely hope that after this—this difficult problem is settled and over, I hope that we—you and I—can resume our friendship. I would very much like to—" Hamilton halted then smiled. "A lawyer is very seldom at a loss for words. It is our stock in trade. Yet, I find myself unable, at this moment, to say what I would like—what is on the tip of my tongue to say—"

For a seemingly endless moment, they looked at each other. The eagerness in his expression, the hope in his eyes, quite silenced anything Nell might have chosen to say in response. She was very conscious of his nearness, the smile that slightly parted his lips. He took off his hat and leaned toward her. If she had not drawn back an inch or two, perhaps their parting would have ended in a kiss. The possibility of that was both thrilling and disturbing.

"Good-bye, Mr. Lewis," Nell said breathlessly. "Thank you very much for the ride and for everything else." She stepped down from the buggy.

"Miss Winston, Nell—" Hamilton said.

At his use of her first name, Nell turned around.

Hamilton seemed about to say something more but said only, "Be careful, please."

"Yes, of course," she replied. With a wave of her hand, she hurried up the path that led past the stable and up to the house.

Nell rushed into the house, up the stairs. She would have

to contact Carrick at once, tell him what she now knew. In her bedroom, Nell sat down at her desk and dashed off a note to Carrick. From what Gervase had said, Dr. Herbert was ready to carry out his plan.

With a mind suddenly wiped clear of any illusion, Nell realized Allegra was in terrible danger. If Dr. Herbert had his way, he could spirit Allegra out of the country, and Desmond would be free to take over the estate. There would be nothing Gervase could do. But if Carrick and Allegra married, all her property would be in his name as her husband. Carrick must move immediately, get Allegra away at once. They could wait no longer. Whatever was to be done had to be done now.

Nell would have to send Jewel with the note to Carrick. Today was the maid's afternoon off; she would serve lunch then leave. Nell would have to find a way to give it to her before she left. With the note burning a hole in her pocket, Nell went downstairs. Only Mrs. Selkirk and a sulky Felicity were in the dining room; Miss Benedict did not appear.

Nell had no appetite. Her stomach felt as quivery as the tomato aspic mold. Felicity, her expression petulant, was indifferently listening to her mother's recital of the clothes she would need for an upcoming house party at a nearby estate. Nell toyed with her salad, trying to catch Jewel's eye with a silent message, but she wasn't sure she was successful.

After lunch, Nell slipped out into the kitchen just in time. Jewel, her shawl on, was tying her bonnet strings and was ready to step out the door. Nell drew her aside, out of earshot of the curious cook and scullery maid. In a hurried whisper she told Jewel, "You must put this note directly into Carrick's hands. No one else's. Understand?"

Jewel's eyes begged more, but Nell could not risk saying anything further.

She saw the girl off with a prayer. She had to trust that Carrick would act on the note. Now, her next step was to get Allegra out of the house before Dr. Herbert had a chance to visit her.

27

*N*ell's breath was coming fast. She raced upstairs and into Allegra's room. Thankfully Wallis was just leaving with her luncheon tray. Allegra usually took a nap at this time of day, before her outing into the garden. Waiting until the door had closed behind Wallis, Nell rushed over to Allegra, took both her hands in hers, leaned close. In a voice that shook with intense excitement, she explained about her meeting with Gervase and all that it meant.

Allegra gasped, turned pale. "Oh, Nell, what can we do? Dr. Herbert is ruthless; he'll do whatever he has to—"

"You're not to worry, Allegra. We'll get you out of here. Carrick is already setting everything in motion. We have a plan. Now, listen; we'll go out to the garden as usual. Everything must look just the same as always. No one must suspect. Carrick will meet us at the dock and—"

"Are you sure? How do you know?"

"I sent Jewel with a note. All we have to do is be there. I'll come and get you when it's time. Remember, act just as you ordinarily would."

That was all Nell had a chance to tell her before Wallis

was back. Nell raised her voice to its normal level. "I'll be back at three, Allegra. It looks like a nice day; we'll get some sunshine."

Giving Allegra's hands a reassuring squeeze, she went out. In the hall, Nell got a glimpse of Miss Benedict. She looked terrible: Her eyes were sunken and dark ringed, her face drawn. The older woman was holding an ice bag in one hand and moving slowly toward her own room. Nell had heard the former governess was prone to migraines; she looked as though she might be suffering from one now and didn't seem to see Nell. For all Miss Benedict's open dislike of her, Nell could not help feeling sorry for her.

However, she had other more pressing things on her mind. She didn't dare contemplate the consequences of what she and Carrick were conspiring to do. Allegra's safety was paramount. Once that was accomplished, they could face anything. Of course, Nell knew her own days at Hope's End were numbered. When Desmond Selkirk discovered she had helped the young couple, he would dismiss her. Even though it was Gervase Montgomery who had hired her and paid her salary, she could only imagine Desmond Selkirk's fury. Maybe she should be prepared to leave with Allegra. But there wasn't time for all the arrangements. Besides, perhaps with Hamilton's assistance, Gervase would clear the legal barriers Selkirk had erroneously contrived. Perhaps even this afternoon they would arrive at Hope's End before either Dr. Herbert or Desmond could act.

Nell's gaze constantly turned to the small clock on the mantel, checking it with her pendant watch; the hands seemed to be moving at a snail's pace. Her mind was barraged with questions. Had Jewel delivered the note? Had Carrick been at home when she came? Did he immediately put the plan into action? So many things could go wrong with even the best-laid plans, and this one had been thrown together at the last minute. Nell wrung her hands.

She checked the window periodically for the slightest

change in the weather. *Please don't let it rain, Lord,* she prayed. Suddenly, Nell saw something that made her heart sink. Dr. Herbert's buggy was rounding the bend of the driveway. It was only two o'clock—two hours earlier than usual and much too early for their plan. As she stared out in stunned horror, the Selkirks' carriage came up close behind. Nell watched as a footman opened the door. Mr. Selkirk got out, accompanied by a shorter man dressed in black and wearing a stovepipe hat. A lawyer? Together they went alongside Dr. Herbert's gig, and the doctor emerged and joined them. The three men stood conferring. What was Desmond doing home from London at this time of day? Did he have legal papers with him giving Dr. Herbert permission to take Allegra to his clinic?

Unable to move and upset by this unexpected turn of events, Nell remained at the window, looking down at the scene. She saw Dr. Herbert motion toward his buggy and the two men walk over to it. The doctor opened the door and assisted a woman out. She wore a starched veil, a blue dress, a short scarlet-lined cape. A nurse! The professional assistant Dr. Herbert had told Miss Benedict he would bring with him when he took Allegra to the clinic.

A surge of energy spun Nell around; she grabbed her jacket and put it on as she ran down the hall to Allegra's room.

Without knocking, Nell hurried in. A quick glance around assured her that, except for Nanny Maybank nodding by the fireplace, no one else was there. Allegra was in the adjoining bedroom, lying on her bed but not asleep. At Nell's entrance, she sat straight up, dropping the book she was reading.

"What is it, Nell?" she gasped.

"Allegra, we must leave right now! There's not a minute to waste! Dr. Herbert is here with a nurse, your uncle Desmond, and a lawyer, I think. We must get you out of here now!"

"But what about Carrick? He won't be there to meet us. Where can we go?"

"I don't know, but we can't take a chance on being caught here. Where are your things?"

Allegra pointed to the coat and fur set that Wallis had already laid out for her.

"Here. Put them on. Can you stand? Lean on me." Shakily, Allegra swung her legs over the side of the bed. Holding on to the bedposts, she got to her feet. Nell picked up the coat and helped her into it, buttoning it. She handed her the muff, placed the hat on her head, and secured the cape with its brocade frogs around her shoulders.

"We don't have time to bring up the wheelchair. Do you think you can walk downstairs?" Nell asked.

Biting her lower lip, her eyes wide with fear, Allegra nodded.

"Wait, let me see if the coast is clear," Nell ordered. She hurried through the sitting room and inched open the door. To her utter dismay, she saw Dr. Herbert just coming to the top of the stairs. Her heart pounded. What now? As she was trying to decide whether to close the door and lock it, she heard Miss Benedict's voice.

"Colin."

Dr. Herbert turned, an annoyed frown on his handsome face.

"You've come—so early, I mean."

His frown deepened. "Yes, what of it? I told you it would only be a matter of days until all the legal transactions were completed. We are going over things now. Desmond has his lawyer; I've brought Sister Jennings—"

"But, Colin, what about me? What about us?"

"What about us?" his tone was mocking.

"I thought—I always thought—"

"I don't know what you're talking about, Clarise."

"Don't say that, Colin. You can't mean that, not after all I've done for you."

"I never made you do anything for me, Clarise. I may have suggested what might be helpful." He paused. "You've been very useful. I've told you that. And you've been compensated for it."

"How? With a few pounds, a few gifts?" Her voice had turned shrill. "I thought I'd have a new life . . . go with you to—"

"Control yourself, Clarise," Dr. Herbert said coldly. "I never led you to believe anyone could make up to me for the loss of Henrietta. The only one who could come close is her daughter. If you thought otherwise, you deluded yourself."

At that Miss Benedict lunged at him. "You cad!" She drew one arm back as if to slap him, but he grabbed her wrist and twisted her arm behind her back.

"Don't be a fool, Clarise." He held her from him for a long moment, then shoved her away. She visibly sagged against the wall, put one shaky hand up to her forehead, then turned and stumbled down the hall toward her bedroom.

Nell was frozen in fear and loathing. Dr. Herbert was frightening. His treatment of Miss Benedict bore out Allegra's story. What cruelty to tell someone that they had been used merely as a means to an end. Of course, it was now clear. He had needed an accomplice. Someone to help him persuade Allegra it would be best for her to go to the clinic. Who better than her former governess, one she trusted and relied on? That had been Clarise's role. Now that the doctor had within his grasp the coveted prize, he was discarding her.

Dr. Herbert took another minute to straighten his collar and adjust his cuffs and was about to continue on toward Allegra's suite when someone called his name. He turned. This time it was Desmond.

"Will you come down again, Colin? Mr. Simmons has a few details he wants to clarify on these papers before we sign them and have Allegra sign them."

To Nell's great relief, Dr. Herbert went back downstairs. She closed the door, locked it with the key, and ran back to Allegra.

"We only have a few minutes. Is there any other way out

of your suite to the lower part of the house?" Nell asked hurriedly.

"Yes. There's a door from the dressing room off my bedroom; it leads to the ironing room, then to the servants' stairs."

"Then that's the way we'll have to go. Can't take a chance of being caught if we use the main stairway. Do you think you can make it?"

"It's awfully steep and narrow." Allegra's lip trembled.

"You'll have to try, Allegra," Nell said firmly. "Come on." She put her arm around Allegra's waist. "Lean on me; I'll steady you. Take one step at a time." They started making a shuffling progress to the door. All of a sudden, Allegra stiffened, halted. "Wait!"

"What's the matter?"

"Tippy!"

In all the confusion, Nell had forgotten about the little dog. She knew they couldn't leave without him. But how could she manage with another unpredictable hindrance to their escape? Quickly she said, "I'll get you to the top of the stairs; you can go down sitting from step to step. And I'll come back and get Tippy."

"Promise?"

"Yes, of course!" Nell said. "Now come on, move."

Nell's heart was pounding. Allegra's slowness was excruciating to her own sense of urgency. Nell was fearful that any moment the business would be completed downstairs and Dr. Herbert, his nurse, Desmond, and his lawyer would mount the steps, come to Allegra's room. What would they do when they found the door locked? Question Wallis? Break in? And would Nell and Allegra have time to get away?

The Yorkie had finally roused from his nap and was sitting up, his pointed ears twitching; he was making little anticipatory sounds as Nell came flying back into the room. She usually rattled the leash to let him know they were going for a walk, but this time she just scooped him up, tucked him under one arm, and ran back to the head of the servants' staircase.

Allegra was more than halfway down. Nell rushed by her, thrusting Tippy onto her lap as she did. "I'll go get the wheelchair from the cloakroom," she said breathlessly and ran the rest of the way down.

Nell wrested the chair from its usual place and had it ready when Allegra reached the bottom of the stairs. She had Tippy cuddled close and was able, with Nell's assistance, to make the transfer into the wheelchair. Nell pushed the chair through the room and out into the garden. Thank heavens they hadn't encountered anyone. Once on the gravel path, Nell pushed harder and faster, praying that Carrick had acted upon her message and would be waiting.

Too impatient to spend the waiting hours at home, too anxious to see his beloved, Carrick had come early. At their appearance, unexpected as it was, he came out from his hiding place at once, kissed Allegra tenderly, then in a low, intense voice said, "I contacted Gervase at The Red Fox Inn like you said. He has been acting on your behalf, Allegra, to prevent Dr. Herbert's taking you to his clinic. It's going to be all right; you're not to worry. I'm going to take you home with me. My mother and stepfather are in complete agreement that this is the right thing to do until Gervase can settle the guardianship matter.

"Now, you're not to be frightened. Nothing can hurt you as long as I'm here. We know you have been in danger. And we are going to find out who is behind it all."

"But how?" Allegra looked from one to the other.

"Nell is going to trade places with you. She is going to put on your hat and cape and sit in the wheelchair. If anyone tries anything, we will be witnesses."

When they got beyond the bend where they could not be seen from the house, the transfer was made. Carrick lifted Allegra gently out of the chair into his arms. Quickly Allegra gave Nell the hat, muff, and cape. Nell put on the hat and cape; then, taking the muff, she sat down in the wheelchair, facing the lake.

"Good-bye and God bless," she whispered to Allegra.

"Are you sure you'll be all right?" Allegra asked worriedly.

"Yes, and we'll know for sure who is the one," Nell said. "Now, go on, you will be safe, and Carrick will come back and watch me from the bushes."

They left, and Nell snuggled deeper into the soft warmth of the sable collar. Maybe this was a crazy stunt. But hadn't she thought it through? Didn't it make sense that someone wanted to get rid of Allegra? At least three people felt they would be better off if she were out of the way. Desmond, certainly. And Felicity, who would be free to marry whomever she wished if saving the family was not necessary. Clarise? Someone had deadly intent and was still trying to carry it out. All they needed was proof.

All these random thoughts raced through Nell's mind as she sat there in the wheelchair staring at the lake; the sun on it was dazzlingly beautiful, its smooth surface serene. However, a paralyzed person could drown easily in its depths. Nell began to empathize how helpless Allegra must have felt all these months, alone with her grief, her knowledge of Dr. Herbert's threats, her inability to speak or move. Nell almost felt the stiffening of her own lower body. Then, she tensed. Behind her she heard stealthy footsteps on the gravel path. Her hands gripped the arms of the wheelchair. Her heart leapt in her chest. Someone was sneaking up, closer and closer. Suddenly she heard the snap of the brake being released; the back of the chair was shaken, given a strong push so quick and with such thrust she had no time to brace herself to keep from falling forward. Propelled, the wheelchair started rocking down the pebbly path to the wooden dock. That apparently was the intent—to send the chair ricketing downhill so fast there would be no way to stop, and it would plunge its helpless occupant into the water.

With a frantic motion of self-preservation, Nell put one

foot over the footrest to halt the speed of the careening wheelchair. In so doing she caused it to tilt sideways, and she fell out. She hit the ground with tremendous force, felt the crunch of her shoulder that took the brunt of the fall, felt the tiny gravel stones cut into her cheek, scrape her forehead. The muff had gone flying as she put out her hands to break her fall, and she sprawled flat. The heavy wheelchair toppled onto her, trapping her underneath, its wheels whirring as they spun.

Nell tried to raise herself on her elbows and free herself from the wheelchair so she could look back and see her attacker. But it was too late. All she saw was the fanlike swirl of the gray tweed ulster as whoever was wearing it fled the scene. Anyone could have worn the ulster. It was always hanging at the door to the garden.

She again tried to pull herself up, but the overturned wheelchair kept her trapped. Leaning on her elbows, she wondered, *Where is Carrick?*

Then she heard a piercing scream. It was Felicity's. "Help, help! Somebody's tried to kill Allegra! Papa, Dr. Herbert, come! They tried to push her off the dock!"

Nell, unable to extricate herself, collapsed back on the ground, lying there prone hearing the pounding of booted feet running on the gravel path, coming nearer, coming to her rescue. She whispered a prayer that Carrick and Allegra had gotten away safely. Then she waited.

She could hear Felicity sobbing hysterically. "I saw her do it! I was just coming up from the stable on the shortcut when I came face-to-face with her on the path. I tried to grab the ulster but she tore loose. . . ."

"Be quiet, girl!" came Desmond's exasperated voice. "Who did you see? Who was it?"

More gulping sobs. "It was—it was—oh, Papa, you won't believe this, but it was Miss Benedict."

Just then the wheelchair was yanked away, freeing Nell. With effort, she raised herself and looked up into Dr. Herbert's face. When he saw it was Nell instead of Allegra, he turned a ghastly white, a gray white. His eyes narrowed then flashed angrily. In the look he and Nell exchanged, he knew that he had been found out, and his eyes turned into those of a wild animal caught in a trap.

Wallis and Lawrence came running and helped Nell to her feet. Carrick, his arm protectively around Allegra, appeared. Then Nell saw Gervase Montgomery and Hamilton coming down from the driveway.

Thank God, she breathed. It was now out of her hands. Others would take over.

This is my last night at Hope's End. It is hard to believe—so much has happened, so many changes have taken place in the months since I first came here. As I packed my things tonight in readiness for my departure tomorrow, I remembered how unwelcome I felt upon my arrival and how subsequent events gradually revealed why.

The house is strangely quiet with most of the occupants gone. After I finished packing, I opened my Bible. I thought of that strangely prophetic passage I read on my first night here: Mark 4:22.

I have no idea what lies ahead of me now. My future seems uncertain, but I believe the Scripture passage I just read: "All things work together for good to them that love God" (Rom. 8:28). I trust that will be true for me.

Nell stood in the downstairs hall, surrounded by her luggage, waiting for the carriage to be brought around to take her to the train station. Her two suitcases, valise, small trunk, and hatbox were all in a neat pile beside her. Oddly enough, she was wearing the same outfit she had worn when she arrived here months ago—the black-and-white Shepherd's check coat with the black velvet collar and cuffs, the bonnet with its curled blue feathers and Alsatian bow with its streaming ribbons. So much was the same, but so much had changed.

Nell felt a sense of satisfaction. She had accomplished what she had been sent here to do. Only the day before, she had seen a radiant, fully recovered Allegra and Carrick off on their honeymoon—a year in the Italian sunshine. She smiled, remembering the happiness of the young couple embarking on a lifetime of love together.

As for herself, Nell felt an inner excitement of what the future might hold. With the more than generous bonus Gervase Montgomery added to her salary, as well as Allegra's own unexpected financial gift, all sorts of possibilities stretched temptingly.

Nell had come here with some expectations, but she had never bargained for what she had found here: hostility she had never before experienced, attempts on her life. Yet, in herself, she had found unexpected courage to act decisively in desperate circumstances. Her whole outlook on life had changed, had broadened, and she was now looking forward to new adventures.

The previous week, Nell had written out an advertisement to place in the *London Times* newspaper. She had spent a great deal of time wording it carefully.

Refined, well-educated young lady, fluent in French, social graces, versed in the classics, cognizant of art, music, opera, is available as a traveling companion. Excellent references. Please send description of position offered, salary, date of travel plans, to:

Here Nell gave her aunts' address where she could be reached, having planned to visit them upon her departure.

If no offers turned up immediately, Nell was going on to France to visit Grandmere. The money Gervase and Allegra had given her provided her with a few months of leisure. She could afford to wait for just the right opportunity for employment. Of course, she could always go back to the Seaview Inn, if it came to that. But surely, something more interesting would come as a result of her advertisement.

There was no one to see her off except Farnsworth and Jewel, who remained to take care of Nanny until the newlyweds returned. The Selkirks, with Mrs. Russell and Mrs. Ellison, had departed to London for the season. A season where they would not have their daughter as a bargaining chip, Nell thought with wry amusement. Felicity had eloped with Douglass and had gone with him to Scotland where he was to take up a new position as stable master for a wealthy laird.

Both Dr. Herbert and Miss Benedict were in jail awaiting trial—he for breaking the physician's oath, for neglecting his duty as a physician, and she for conspiracy and attempted murder. They would both be in prison for a long time.

Even though both deserved their punishment, Nell could not help thinking it ironic that love, or a distorted kind of love, an obsession, had brought them both to this deplorable fate.

"The carriage is here, miss." Farnsworth's voice interrupted Nell's sobering retrospect of recent events.

"Good-bye, Farnsworth," she said as he opened the front door for her.

"Good-bye, miss, and Godspeed."

Nell was feeling especially optimistic as she settled into the cushioned seat of the carriage. As they started off, she turned to take a last look at the house through the back window. A house of shadows, it truly was. Heavy vines nearly obscured the windows, and the slanting roof darkened the curtained windows of the second floor. Its facade sheltered many mysteries. Nell felt a tiny shiver. She would leave

Hope's End to its secrets, its dark corridors, and its hidden hallways. Nell turned and faced forward, glad to leave it all behind.

Seated in her old bedroom, Nell was contentedly looking through *Lady's Gazette* when a tap came at the door. Tilly, the aunts' pink-cheeked maid, stuck her head in, announcing in an awed tone, "A gentleman to see you, miss."

Nell looked up from her fashion magazine. "A gentleman?"

"Yes, miss. He said you might be expecting him."

Nell frowned. Who could it be? Gervase? She hoped that nothing had gone wrong, that there was no bad news from the honeymooners.

She got up quickly, letting the magazine slip from her lap to the floor. This was her aunts' at-home day, and Nell had dressed appropriately. Still, she took a quick, reassuring look in her bureau mirror before going downstairs. A creamy ruffle of lace emerged from the neck of a fitted, velvet jacket the color of crushed grapes, and a darker plum skirt flared from her small waist.

Nell knew her aunts had invited several of their acquaintances for tea. This must be an early arrival. However, when she entered the small parlor, she couldn't have been more astonished to see Hamilton Lewis standing in front of the fireplace. All the reserve of proper etiquette vanished in her rush of surprise, and she gasped, "What are you doing here?"

He smiled, and she was newly aware of the sparkle in his eyes, the humorous tilt of his mouth. Regarding her carefully, he drew a folded bit of paper out of the pocket of his waistcoat and held it out to her. "I've come in answer to an advertisement in the *London Times*." His smile had more than a hint of mischief as he glanced down at the slip of paper and read, "I'm looking for a refined, well-educated young lady, fluent in French, versed in the classics, cognizant of art, etcetera, etcetera—as a traveling companion." He paused, then took three deliberate steps toward Nell, who was standing completely still.

Hamilton was now so close that his eyes were almost level with her own. "I want to offer this young lady a position, a permanent one. Have I found her?" His eyebrows lifted. "Will you, my dear Miss Nell Winston, accept what I'm offering?"

As Hamilton waited for Nell's answer, the ticking of the clock on the mantelpiece seemed very loud in the quiet parlor.

"Nell." He said her name, then again, "Nell?"

She saw humor, tenderness, hope, and a little anxiety mingled in his eyes. Very softly he said, "I love you, Nell."

Then he held out his arms, and she went into them.

Epilogue

September 3, 1894

I can hardly believe what I am about to write in the last few pages of this book, which I started a year ago. When I went to Hope's End, I had no idea what to expect and never bargained for what I found there. However, I did not dream that my life would be unalterably changed.

When I return from a visit to see Grandmere, Hamilton Lewis and I will be married at his family's estate. Lady Anne has insisted on our having the wedding there.

Afterwards we shall leave on a year-long honeymoon. Hamilton has it all arranged. We are going to Egypt first. He says he began to plan it after our first conversation at Hope's End. "I fell in love with you that first night," he tells me. "And then after we began to talk I knew I had found my life's companion." So much has happened since Hamilton came here in April. I had not the faintest hint that it would all end so marvelously. The aunts adore him, and, when I am at Grandmere's, he will come over to meet her.

For most of my life, I have set out on journeys alone. As a child, I left for my annual summer visit in France and returned in the fall to school with my aunts. I was always given my ticket, a small amount of money for unexpected need, instructions of just where to go, what to say and do, not to talk to strangers, and where to get off. This will be the last venture in which I will do so.

When I come back from my visit to Grandmere, there will be someone meeting me, someone who loves me, someone with whom I will set out on my most important journey.

Love awaits me, life awaits me. Au revoir.

Jane Peart is a prolific author of romantic fiction who lives in Fortuna, California. She is the author of the Orphan Train West series and the International Romance series.